BEECH b.

Beech Bank Girls

# *Every Girl Has a Story*

### ELEANOR WATKINS

DERNIER PUBLISHING
Tonbridge

First published 2009

Published by Dernier Publishing
P.O. Box 403, Tonbridge, TN9 9BJ, England
<www.dernierpublishing.com>

ISBN  978 0 9536963 4 5

*Cover illustration copyright © by Alison Blackwell*

Book design and production for the publisher by
Bookprint Creative Services, <www.bookprint.co.uk>
Printed in Great Britain.

To my granddaughters
Lyndsay, Samantha, Chloe,
three very special girls,
with love

# Contents

# PART ONE

# *Annie's Story*

## RUNNER

# *one*

I didn't really expect to enjoy the first day at my new school, Beechwood High, and I was right. For one thing, the school uniform we'd ordered hadn't come in time, and I had to go in an ordinary navy sweatshirt and jeans. The other girls had proper school sweatshirts with the school logo in gold, and either navy trousers or short navy skirts and black tights. I felt I stuck out like a sore thumb.

Then, it was difficult learning the layout of the school. I'd been used to a huge, modern, glass and steel comprehensive. This school was an old converted mansion house, with lots of staircases, corridors and rooms tucked away by themselves. By the first break I was hopelessly lost. Timetable in hand, I found myself wondering desperately how I was going to find my classroom for the next lesson.

The corridor was deserted. Everyone was safely installed in their own classes. Then I heard hurrying footsteps. A small, dark girl skidded to a halt beside me.

"You lost?"

I nodded, blushing. How I wished I could get out of

that stupid blushing habit. I bent my head and let my hair fall forward to hide my face.

The girl sounded friendly. And she was in my class. I'd noticed her that morning with a group of others. I looked into brown eyes in a round, rosy face. She looked friendly, but you never knew.

"You're the new girl. Anna, isn't it?"

"Annie," I said.

"Oh yes. I'm Rachel. Just come with me. But we'll have to hurry. I'm late. Had to go back for something I forgot. Come on."

We hurried together down steps and round a corner, and were in the classroom. The teacher was not pleased at our late entrance and made a sarcastic comment to Rachel, who said, "Sorry, Mr Bryce," and slipped meekly into her place.

Mr Bryce peered at me and what I was wearing, seemed to recall that I was new and waved me impatiently to my seat. "Just sit, girl."

My cheeks were still warm, and I felt that everyone must be thinking that I was a complete dork. I sat, and tried to concentrate.

At lunchtime I saw Rachel again, with a group of four or five others. Everyone seemed to be in a group as they queued up at the lunch counter. One or two of them glanced at me and made a comment between themselves. Somebody jogged my arm while I was holding out my plate for gravy, and someone else sniggered. It could have been an accident, of course. But there'd been so many incidents like that at the last school that I wasn't giving anyone the benefit of the doubt.

I moved off and found a table in a corner, all by myself, until a couple of year seven boys came and sat opposite because there was no room anywhere else. Their table manners were gross, and after a while they started showing off, telling each other stupid jokes and flicking bits of food about. I ignored them, staring miserably out into the chattering crowds at the other tables. Rachel and her friends were at the opposite end of the dining hall, talking and laughing. One of the girls in the group was tall and slim, and had a mass of red hair that made her stand out. Another was blonde. They were having a great time. What I'd give to be part of a group like that, to talk to and hang out with. But I hadn't a hope.

Suddenly, Rachel turned a little and saw me staring at her. She said something to the others. All of them turned and looked. Then, to my horror, they started pushing back their chairs and getting to their feet. They were coming over to my corner.

I jumped up so quickly that the two year sevens stopped their idiotic chatter and stared at me. I left the last bit of cottage pie uneaten and headed for the door nearby. It led to yet another corridor, which I hurried along until the dining hall chatter dimmed in my ears. At the far end, another door led to what seemed to be a large storeroom, with cupboards and stacked-up crates and boxes. I sat on a large wooden crate containing cans of baked beans, put my hot face into my hands and had a little weep. Why did I have to be such an idiot?

I stayed in the storeroom until the next period began, and no one seemed to take any notice of me for the rest of the afternoon. I was so glad the new house was in walking distance of school and I wouldn't have to travel on the school bus.

Mum was in the hallway, unpacking boxes. She asked, "Good day, dear? How was the new school? Oh, by the way, your uniform's come."

I said something non-committal and headed straight upstairs. The school was okay, the other kids no worse than any. It's me that doesn't fit anywhere, I thought miserably.

"Come and have a cup of tea and tell me about it," Mum called up from below.

My room was a jumble of hastily dumped possessions. My eight-year-old brother Harry was home from school, I could hear pinging sounds from his room as he played a computer game. I took a pile of his clothes that someone had dumped in my room and carried them to his. It looked like a bomb site; stuff strewn everywhere as he sat absorbed in his game. I guessed he'd been sent up to put things away. He grinned up at me, blue eyes serene. His day at the new primary school had been okay. Harry never let new schools or anything else get him down for long. I wished I was more like him.

Going back to my own room, I heard the garden gate click. Through the landing window I saw –

horrors! – a group of girls, still in school uniform, trooping up the path. One was small and dark, another had flame-red hair.

Quick as a flash I grabbed my bathrobe and dived across the landing into the bathroom as the doorbell rang. I put in the plug and turned both taps full on. My heart hammered. Rashly I poured bubble bath into the tub, then jumped as a knock came at the door. "Annie?" Mum's voice sounded puzzled. "Are you in there? There are some girls here asking for you."

"Sorry." I could hear how my voice sounded, strange and squeaky. "I'm just having a bath."

I heard her go downstairs. I like a nice power shower in the mornings, and don't do baths, usually. But the tub was full of bubbles and I had to fill in the time until the girls went away. I undressed and got in.

In spite of myself I felt some of the day's tensions drain away as I lay and soaked. I hoped the girls wouldn't decide to wait. I didn't know why they'd come. Rachel had seemed friendly, but girls were different in a group – or a pack, as I sometimes thought about them. I remembered the last school and shuddered. That was what it had been like – a quarry hunted down by a pack of bullies. I'd been told bullies backed off when one stood up to them, but the one time I'd tried I'd ended up with a split lip and a torn shirt. I'd never told. The bullies had only stopped because we'd moved. And I was still scared.

I soaked in the bath, half dozing, until Mum

banged on the door again. "Annie? Are you all right in there?"

"Yes, Mum. Just coming." I wallowed my way out of the bath, dried off, and came out to find Mum putting away towels in the landing cupboard. She looked at my pink, shiny face and damp hair in a puzzled way. "I thought you didn't take baths. Just showers." Her face was troubled; it often was nowadays.

"Well, I've changed," I said. "It's allowed, isn't it?"

"Of course." She seemed surprised at my crabby tone. "By the way, four or five girls from your school were here. From your year, I think. Wanted to know if you'd like to go out for a bit. A shame you missed them."

My heart leapt, torn between hope and doubt. Had they really meant it? Were they to be trusted?

The doubt won. I shrugged, and took a clean towel from the pile to dry my hair. "Couldn't have gone, anyway. Homework," I said, and marched off to my room before she could say more. I felt her looking after me, concerned and mystified. I knew she wished I'd have a cup of tea and talk to her. Part of me wanted to go back and fling myself into her arms and tell her my hopes and fears, and ask why I couldn't be like other girls, with real friends to hang out with. I closed my door with a snap, plugged in my DVD player and put in a CD with the kind of beat that Mum said gave her a headache. It made me forget my troubles for a bit, and it was also good for covering up any embarrassing sounds, like the odd sob or two.

# *two*

The next school day started much the same as the first one, except that I now had a school uniform, which I hoped would help me merge into the background. I avoided the group with Rachel, the red-haired girl, the fair one and the couple of others who seemed to be part of the gang. A few of the class – including a cool-looking boy – said hi in passing, but I didn't encourage more talk. The redhead – Willow – asked if I was settling in okay and I said, "Yes, thanks," and left it at that. When a couple of others in the group smiled at me, I ducked my head and pretended not to see.

At lunchtime I sat in my corner again, making sure Rachel and Willow's group were settled far enough away. Part of me was kicking myself for this stupid behaviour. The girls had shown no sign of being anything but friendly. But I knew from bitter experience how quickly that friendliness could turn to sheer bitchy nastiness, or worse.

Lunch over, I made myself scarce, deciding to walk around the building refreshing my memory about the location of classrooms, and so on. I purposely picked the areas with the least people about, but even so I was stared at by those I did see. At last I decided to take refuge again in a quiet place and wait for the start of afternoon lessons. I headed for the storeroom I'd been in yesterday, which seemed to be little used.

This time the door was closed. I stopped as I reached it. A soft buzz of girls' voices came from inside. I was beginning to tiptoe away again, when I heard my name mentioned – I'm sure it was my name, Annie isn't that common. Then another voice chipped in saying something I couldn't hear – and then my name again. My heart began to race. I felt a shiver go down my spine. Whoever they were, they were talking about me! Part of me wanted to listen and the other part wanted to get away fast. I turned sharply, stumbled a little, and lurched with a thud against the door.

The voices stopped and the door flew open. Before I could move, Willow stood there, her hair making a flaming halo round her head. Her mouth fell open in surprise. Behind her, I caught a glimpse of the other girls, sitting on boxes and crates in a close circle, their startled faces turned towards the door.

Willow recovered herself. "Oh – Annie! It's you. Actually, you're just the person we wanted to see. Come in."

I stared at her. Her eyes were very green against her pale skin. My heart thudded hard. Whatever was going on in there, it had something to do with me. Were they planning some kind of bullying, some way of getting me by themselves? To do what?

Wild horses wouldn't have dragged me into that room. I got a grip on myself and backed away down the corridor. One or two of the other girls came to the door. One of them said, "Don't go. Please come and join us."

I was already heading off as fast as I could go. Anywhere, to get away.

"Wait!" said Willow. But I wasn't waiting. Whatever plot they were hatching, I was out of there as fast as I could go. I ran down the corridor, through the dining hall where the tables were being cleared, back to the comparative safety of the front yard.

I noticed one or other of the girls glance at me now and then during afternoon classes. Panic began to well up inside me again. They'd got me marked down for something, and I had no idea what. And I wasn't going to hang around to find out. At home time, I decided on avoidance tactics. They'd followed me home yesterday and might do so again. Mum had started her new job today. I called her on my mobile from the girls' cloakroom.

"Mum? I thought I'd go into town for a bit, have a look around. I'll be about half an hour late."

"Oh – good idea," said Mum. "Some of the others will show you around, I expect. I've arranged for Harry to go home with another boy in his class – Rowan. Maybe you could pick him up? I've got the address here." I heard her smoothing out a bit of paper. "Yes, here it is." She read it out, and said, "It's on your way home. First turn off the main street, end house in the cul-de-sac. Well, have a nice time. And give me a ring when you've collected Harry."

I hung up and sighed. Mum obviously thought I was off to enjoy myself with new friends. If only it were true.

The new town was quite different to the one I'd lived in before, a small country town after a huge busy one. I wasn't at all sure I liked the fact that everyone seemed to know everyone else here. No chance to hide among big crowds. I spent the next half hour ducking and diving around the shops, doing a disappearing act whenever anyone in a Beechwood High uniform came into view. There were some nice shops; small boutiques, craft shops and interesting bookshops tucked away in little cobbled side streets away from the town centre. But I couldn't appreciate any of them, keeping one eye on my watch and the other out for trouble. It was a relief when it was time to go to pick up Harry.

Rowan's house was easy enough to find, being directly on my route home, a pleasant looking semi with a garden that looked a bit overgrown and neglected. I could hear the sound of boys' voices in an upstairs room before I pressed the bell, yelling and shouting in the way small boys do when they're enjoying themselves. Harry would fit in and make friends wherever he went.

A tall, thin woman in paint-spattered jeans and a smock answered my ring. There was something vaguely familiar about her. She said, "Oh, you must be

Annie! Your mum just called. Come in, and I'll go and sort out those two terrors."

She chattered away, shutting the door behind me. "I hope you're all settling in. Rowan and Harry seem to be best mates already. You must be in my daughter's year at the High School. She's doing homework in the kitchen – come on through."

Warning bells began to ring in my mind, but she was ushering me through a door and into a pleasant but untidy kitchen. There was a smell of coffee and something was bubbling on the cooker. School books were spread over the table, and a pair of startled green eyes in a face surrounded by a halo of red hair looked up at me.

# *three*

For a moment we just stared at each other, Willow and I. Then she put down her pen and started to laugh. "You're Harry's sister! I don't believe it!" She ran her long slim fingers through her fiery hair and laughed again.

I felt trapped, standing there wordless. It seemed that fate had played a cruel trick. I'd struggled to avoid Willow and her mates in every way I could, and now I'd fetched up right on her doorstep. And I couldn't turn and run away because of Harry.

Willow's green eyes were gleaming – in triumph, I thought. She nodded towards the chair opposite and said, "Sit down."

I sat, heart thudding. She got up and went over to the stove. "Coffee? It's proper coffee, not instant. I can't cope with homework straight after school without a good strong coffee."

I took the mug warily. I didn't trust her. I hardly sipped the coffee. For all I knew she might have put something into it. I knew that she and her friends were planning something. Once, the bullies at the other school had dissolved a laxative in my hot chocolate. I still remembered the humiliation. Nothing like that was going to happen to me again.

I knew this was a stupid way of thinking, but my good sense seemed to have completely gone. She poured herself a coffee, strong and black. "That's better. Well, Annie, this is nice. We did call round to yours after school yesterday. Did your mum tell you?"

I nodded.

"Thought we'd like to know you better. We were going to see if you wanted to come out with us for a bit. There's a club we go to after school sometimes. Or a gang of us go shopping on Saturdays. Or get together for homework."

It all sounded cool. But then, those other girls had been cool too, in the beginning, until they found how easily they could freak me out. I gulped, and found my voice.

"I'm a bit busy. Unpacking, and all that stuff."

She seemed to accept the feeble excuse. Voices sounded from upstairs. I willed them to come down, wanting to get Harry and escape from there. Willow got up and wandered to the window, holding her mug. I noticed how tall and slim she was. Willowy. Her name suited her. She'd changed her uniform for designer jeans and a little crop top, and her trainers were a brand most girls my age would kill for. She seemed thoughtful for a moment, and then came back and sat opposite me again. "Look, Annie, it's Chloe's birthday in a few weeks. Chloe's the blonde one. Anyway, she's not too happy at the moment. Family stuff. The rest of us thought we'd give her a party. Could you come?"

I gulped again. How was I going to get out of this one? I nodded and found myself saying, "Er —well, thanks." I'd have to find some excuse to get out of it before the day came. She leaned towards me confidentially. I could see there was more.

And then the two small boys came bursting into the room, followed by Willow's mum. Willow looked slightly annoyed. She'd wanted me to herself for a bit longer.

I leapt up, almost spilling the untouched coffee. "Oh, finish your coffee," said Willow's mum. "There's no hurry, is there?"

"We have to go," I gabbled, and grabbed Harry's hand. "Thanks for having him."

As I shouldered both our bags and headed for the door, I noticed in the hall mirror that Willow and her mother exchanged a look. They probably thought me well strange. Well, they were right. I was strange. Strange and sad. And lonely. I hadn't fitted in before and I didn't fit here either.

I got home feeling exhausted and stressed-out. Mum was home from work already, sitting near the phone in the kitchen, surrounded by half-unpacked crates and boxes. She looked exhausted too. I had the feeling she'd been crying.

"Mum? Was the job awful?"

She tried to pull herself together. "The job? Oh no, the job was fine. Better than my old one." She pushed a hand through her hair, looked around at the muddle and seemed to make up her mind. "Come and sit down for a minute, both of you."

I knew something was coming and tried to put off the moment. "Mum? Shall I make a cup of tea? I'll help you sort out things later. You'll feel better when things are straight." I was babbling on like an idiot, trying to pretend nothing was really wrong, when I knew it was. "It'll look fine when all this stuff's put away. And we can get the big furniture sorted when Dad comes at the weekend."

Mum looked at me. She pulled Harry onto her lap and he helped himself to a chocolate biscuit from a packet on the table. She said, "That's what I have to tell you. Dad isn't coming."

Both of us stared at her. Harry said, "You mean not ever?"

Mum said, "No. Not ever."

Harry kept staring, his mouth full of biscuit crumbs. Mum went on, sounding tired and flat, "I hoped that moving here would be a fresh start for all of us. But it's not going to happen. He's not coming. We're going to live apart."

"Divorce?" I asked. Mum just nodded.

Harry's eyes filled with tears and he began to bawl. "I want him to come! I want Dad!"

Mum and I looked at each other over his head. I'd known they weren't getting on. I'd had a feeling this might happen, but I'd tried to block it out, not think about it. To run away, I suppose, which was always my pathetic way of handling things. Harry was sobbing into Mum's shoulder, smearing chocolate and snotty tears into her navy silk work blouse. She said, appealing to us both, "You'll both be able to see him regularly. And he'll go on supporting us financially. In fact, he's raising your allowances . . ."

Oh, great! So a few pounds extra pocket money will make up for him running out on us! I didn't say the words, but I had a horrid bitter, empty feeling inside. Even my Dad thinks I'm not worth the bother.

One part of me knew that once again I wasn't thinking straight, and that Mum needed understanding and support too. Well, too bad. It was asking too much just now.

"I could do with that cup of tea, love," said Mum bleakly.

"In a minute," I mumbled, and turned and made for the stairs, before the tears started pouring down my cheeks. Yesterday had been a bad day, but today must rate as the worst ever.

## *four*

The worst day, followed by the worst night. I couldn't eat any tea, though Harry had recovered by then, and shovelled in as much chilli and rice as usual. I went to bed early, and lay awake hours after I heard Mum go upstairs and into her lonely room. How could Dad do this to us? All of us needed him. As Mum said, this move had been going to be a new start. And now everything was ruined, hopeless. I pulled the duvet over my head and snuffled into my damp pillow.

By the morning, I'd made up my mind about one thing. I couldn't face school, no way, couldn't keep avoiding Willow and Rachel and the others as well as trying to get my head round this thing with Dad. Mum seemed to have got Harry into some kind of after-school club, and she'd pick him up after work. As for me, I was bunking off.

I'd never done this before, no matter how bad things

had been. I'd never dared. But being new made it easier to swing it. I didn't want the school ringing Mum, so I put on my uniform, took my school stuff, walked to school and went to registration. Then, instead of going to the first class, I simply melted away in the crowd and dodged towards a side entrance and freedom.

It was surprisingly easy. No one seemed to notice me leaving. I got into town, went into the toilets near the car park and changed into the tracksuit I'd stuffed into my rucksack.

Just being away from school made me feel better. It was warm for October, and I'd put my sunglasses into my bag too. With shades on, my hair pulled back into a ponytail and a baseball cap on, I looked a totally different girl to the one who'd set out that morning. I was beginning to feel much better.

I spent the morning exploring the town at my leisure, looking at clothes in the little boutiques, thumbing through books in the bookshops, finding my way about the twisty little streets. Lots of touristy people were about and no one took any notice of me at all. At lunchtime I treated myself to a bowl of pasta and an espresso coffee in a cool restaurant. Then I wandered into a kind of park area, with trees and bushes, winding paths, and a small lake with lots of quacking ducks. It was really warm by now. I tossed crisps to the ducks for a bit, and then sat down on the grass near a rhododendron bush. Beyond the park sounded the muffled hum of the town. The sleepless night was catching up with me. I yawned a few times, then lay down with my head on my rucksack and fell asleep in the shade.

I woke with a crick in the neck. Sitting up and rubbing my neck with both hands, I saw that someone was sitting on the seat a few yards away, watching the ducks. It was a man, about forty, with longish dark hair and one of those padded lumberjack shirts. He looked across at me and smiled. "Hello there. Had a good nap?"

"Yes, thanks." I got up stiffly, blushing with embarrassment to think that someone had been watching me as I slept. How long had I been asleep anyway? With relief, I saw from my watch that school wouldn't be finished quite yet. I'd have time to get home before any kids from Beechwood High appeared.

"You live round here?" the man was asking. He had blue eyes that crinkled at the corner and a nice smile.

I nodded. I knew I shouldn't be talking to strange men, but this one seemed harmless enough. And it was broad daylight, in a public place. Some mums and toddlers were feeding the ducks, and a couple of old men were on another seat just yards away.

"A nice town," he said. "Very friendly people."

I nodded again, shouldering my rucksack. I'd go home, get changed, and be ready for when Mum and Harry came. Maybe I'd get dinner started. I'd been sulky and grumpy that morning. It wasn't Mum's fault after all, what had happened. I'd try and be nice.

When Mum and Harry got home I had school books

spread out and a story ready if questions were asked. I didn't need it though. Harry was his chirpy self again and full of enthusiasm about the after-school club. Mum seemed more cheerful, too, now that things were in the open. She was well impressed with the defrosted chops and peeled vegetables I'd done, relieved that all of us were on a more even keel. I felt my own spirits lifting.

Maybe she and Dad would be able to get things sorted. People did get back together after splitting up. Maybe they could go to Relate or counselling or something like that.

I didn't want to think about school. Tomorrow was Friday and then it would be the weekend. I'd get through each day as it came.

Next day I followed the same routine – off to school in uniform, registration, bunk off into town and change clothes. It was getting harder though. I felt I got one or two strange looks at school, though no one stopped me or said anything. The day in town wasn't quite as good as yesterday's either. Same shops, same boutiques with same clothes, same streets, same tourists. This could get boring after a while. Better than school though. I had fish and chips for lunch and then went to the park.

Same ducks in the same lake, the same mums and toddlers, same old people on seats. And after a while, the same man.

He appeared from behind me as I sat on the seat by the lake reading, and sat down beside me.

"Hello again."

I wasn't too keen on him sitting beside me, but thought it would seem rude to get up and walk off, especially as I'd spoken to him yesterday. So I said, "Oh, hello," and went on reading.

"Interesting book?" He'd moved up a couple of inches to try and see what I was reading. I could smell him, a kind of sweaty tobacco-ish smell, and I didn't like being that close. I nodded and inched away. I was beginning to remember all the stories I'd heard about perverts. This man didn't seem like one though. Although – he'd moved up again, and suddenly there was no more room. I'd reached the end of the seat. And then he was reaching out a hand towards my knee.

For a split second I froze, staring at the hand, which had a scar on the thumb and grimy broken fingernails. Then in one leap I was off the seat, dropping the book, clutching my rucksack and running like crazy across the grass, through the bushes, anywhere to escape.

## *five*

I burst out from the trees and bushes as though all the monsters in creation were after me. As it happened, nobody was at all. The creepy man had not followed.

Just the same, I was petrified. I half-fell out of

the rhododendrons into the roadway, right into the middle of a group of girls in school uniform walking along together.

It was Willow, Rachel, Chloe and a couple of others. All of them stopped and stared at my wild eyes, messy hair and a long scratch where a bramble twig had caught my cheek. Then someone said, "It's Annie!" and someone else said, "Whatever's happened?" Then arms and hands were reaching out to me, not threateningly, but steadying and comforting and reassuring. I found myself sobbing on Willow's shoulder with her arms holding me tight, while the others patted and stroked and made clucking "there, there" kinds of sounds. In between sobs, I blurted out the story of the man in the park. They tut-tutted some more.

"Some pervy creep," said Rachel. "But it's okay. You're safe now."

And I was. Suddenly I knew it. I was safe. Safe and comforted and cared for. When I really looked into the girls' eyes, I could see that they meant what they were saying. I'd been all wrong about them. Running like a scared rabbit when there was no reason to run. There in the roadway they mopped my tears, straightened my cap, which had gone askew, dusted me down and dabbed at my scratched cheek. I took a few deep breaths (Willow's suggestion) and then found myself explaining everything – how I'd been a shy kid bullied at my old school, how I was scared of being bullied again and how I'd bunked off school. I even mentioned a bit about my dad leaving, and with every breath I felt lighter and more free.

"Poor you!" said Willow at last. "And fancy being scared of us! Tell you what, why don't you come along with us and have a coffee? You could text your mum and let her know."

"We're going to the Beech Bank Club," said Chloe. "It's open after school – we go quite often. It's cool. You'll like it."

And there I was, walking along with a group of girls, arm-in-arm with two of them, accepted and wanted and comforted, with a new warm fuzzy feeling welling up inside me.

The Beech Bank Club turned out to be a kind of youth group held in the Community Centre at the end of Beech Avenue. Lots of things seemed to be going on as we went in. Two boys, one of whom I recognised from school, were playing pool at a table in the big lobby area. I heard the plink, plonk of table-tennis from somewhere else. A TV screen flickered from the doorway of a smaller room and I glimpsed people sitting at computers through another doorway. The girls hurried me along to a large kitchen, with an adjoining café area like a little bistro, with red checked tablecloths on the round tables. One or two groups were drinking coffee and generally chilling out.

A tall, attractive woman was standing in the kitchen area, clutching a coffee mug and chatting to a couple of girls. All of them were laughing over something one

of them had said. The tall woman greeted Willow and
the others, and then noticed me. "Oh, someone new.
Great! I'm Sadie Harris. Would you like coffee?"

Willow introduced me, and added, "Sadie and Rod,
her husband, run this place. Let's go in the snug. It'll
be quieter there."

The snug turned out to be just what it sounded,
a small cosy room with comfy armchairs. The six of
us ensconced ourselves there and sat down with our
coffee mugs. I'd learned the names of the other two
now – Holly was brown-haired and pretty, Amber
quite noisy, you could tell she liked to be the centre of
attention, but nice. All of them seemed thrilled to bits
to have me there with them.

I felt the warm feeling spreading and expanding,
melting the knot of fear and distrust that I'd carried
around for so long. I was beginning to relax, with the
amazing feeling that at last I was being accepted, even
welcomed, as part of a group.

"I'm just so sorry," said Willow, looking at me over
her black coffee. "I mean, that we frightened you."

"It's all right," I said quickly. "It was just – well –
because of what happened before."

Several of them nodded. "It explains a lot. Why you
were always running away. It seemed so weird."

"Maybe we seemed weird too," said Willow quickly.
"For instance, that day in the storeroom."

I'd been wondering about that too. I put down my
mug carefully and said, quite surprised at my own

boldness, "Well, I did hear my name mentioned. More than once. You *were* talking about me, weren't you? I heard my name."

The girls looked at each other and then at Willow, who seemed to be their leader and spokesperson. She said, "Well, yes. Not talking, though, exactly. I mean, not gossiping or slagging you off. We were praying."

I shot bolt upright as though someone had stuck a pin into me. Praying? At lunchtime? In *school*? Not even in a church? My gran goes to church and presumably prays, but I'd never heard of anything like this before.

Willow seemed to be reading my thoughts because she said, "You can pray anywhere. Doesn't have to be in a church. It's just talking to God. You can do it wherever you are. The school lets us have that room for our prayer-group once a week."

I gulped. This was *seriously* weird. She seemed to be saying that you could talk to God just like he's another person. That she and the others did just that. And where did I come into all this?

Willow was explaining, "We noticed you that first day in school. You looked kind of lonely and really scared. We couldn't seem to get to talk to you to make friends. So we decided we'd pray about it. About you. It was just chance that you overheard."

"Or maybe not," added Rachel mysteriously.

My head was reeling. These girls really believed what they were saying. That God is real. That he's interested in everyone – even me. I couldn't quite take it all in. I didn't know what to say. Looking round the room for inspiration, my eye fell on a poster on the wall, a bright picture of a singing blackbird, with a caption saying, "*Let everything that has breath praise the Lord.*'

I said, "This place, is it, a – a religious club?"

One or two of the girls grinned. Rachel said, "Sadie and Rod wouldn't call it that. But it *is* a Christian one. Rod is the vicar at St John's."

Another shock. Sadie Harris, in her blue jeans, trainers and trendy short haircut, a vicar's wife?

I just didn't know what to make of any of it. This last week had been different to any I'd ever known. I'd thought at times that things were going from bad to worse.

Not any more though. Despite the new ideas, the strange things I'd been told, the things I couldn't quite get my head around, I felt good. I could even think of that weird man in the park as just someone sad and pathetic. I wasn't afraid any more.

I no longer wanted to run.

# PART TWO

# Willow's Story

## DESIGNER STYLE

# one

I was dead chuffed the afternoon that the new girl, Annie, came to the Beech Bank Club for the first time. Me and the others had been trying to get to know her all that week, since she joined our school. She seemed scared of her own shadow, though. Then there was a mystery, because she wasn't in class any more, although Amber was sure she'd seen her at registration. And then, there she was, bursting out from the bushes round the park, crying and shaking, with blood on her face.

I suppose I was the one she'd talked to most, although it hadn't been much more than a dozen words altogether. Anyway, she grabbed hold of me and clung on as though her life depended on it. It was okay, though. She came to Beech Bank with us, and told us all about it, and after a bit you could see she was kind of beginning to unwind and come back to life again.

It's strange the way God answers our prayers. And how he turns really crummy situations around and brings good out of them. And even uses our weak spots to teach us things and make us stronger in the end. Sadie has always said that to us, and I've heard Rod say it in his Sunday sermons too.

I've always thought of myself as a strong person. Rowan and me are the only two children in our family. Mum and Dad are not your traditional parents – in fact, they could be called a bit weird, kind of ancient hippie types. (That's why Rowan and I have these names.) Dad and Mum were eco-warriors back in the '80s and they've never really grown out of it. Then, they had long ringlets (both of them!) wore rainbow jumpers, chained themselves to trees, went barefoot, smoked weed and dropped out. They've toned down a little bit, I suppose, though they support the Green party, go on anti-war marches, consider their carbon footprint, recycle everything, etc, etc. They don't smoke any more (in fact they are against any kind of smoking) and their hair is shorter, but apart from that not much has changed. Except that they work – Dad teaches Humanities at a local school (not ours) and Mum paints and sculpts. I suppose you could call them semi-conformist now. They've taught Rowan and me to be independent and think for ourselves. That includes being able to make our own tea and fend for ourselves. Also not to blindly accept anything we're told. So, I've done just that, thought for myself and decided that I'm not all that keen on their way of thinking and their way of life (though I love them loads).

It was partly because of this that I decided I was going to church. Mum and Dad said we must make up our minds for ourselves, be free to examine and choose from any of the world's religions or to have none. Therefore, to prove my independence, I chose the most traditional one of all, the local C of E. My parents were a bit surprised. I don't think either of them could make out how they'd raised such a square daughter.

Anyway, I went along to a Youth Service one Sunday evening with my friend Holly. It wasn't a bit like I'd expected. The vicar was young, and although he had a dog-collar, he wore it with an ordinary dark jacket and black jeans. His wife, Sadie, was lovely too, and their two little kids were cute as could be. I started going every Sunday.

Pretty soon, something odd seemed to be happening. Every time Rod (the vicar) spoke about Jesus, I'd have this strange feeling inside, this kind of longing to know more. Rod and Sadie were unlike anyone I'd ever known. They were ordinary people in many ways, struggled to make ends meet and worked really hard, long hours. But they talked about Jesus as though he was a friend, and when they prayed, it sounded just like they were talking *to* a friend, a really close one. And yet Jesus was meant to be God's son and part of God himself, who'd created the world and the universe, the sun, moon and stars. It blew my mind away.

I started to ask questions. That was the neat thing about Rod and Sadie, you could ask them anything, tell them anything, and they were cool with it. They told me I could know Jesus for myself, and one day they prayed with me, and I asked Jesus into my heart and my life.

Wow! That was the most amazing day of my life. Suddenly I knew he was there and would never leave me. And for the first time ever, I could be myself, not as others wanted me to be, not even feeling the need to rebel or prove anything to Mum and Dad.

Of course, they were a bit sceptical when I told them. Dad thought it was maybe a religious phase I was going through. (He and Mum had explored Buddhism for a time. They'd discarded it after a while and thought it likely I'd discard my "craze".)

Mum felt I should explore other faiths and not become too narrow. "You don't want to close your mind to other influences," she told me. "The world, the earth and universe hold such wonders, such wonderful things."

But I had found my wonderful thing. I gobbled up all I was taught, went to Bible studies and Christian camps and houseparties and youth events. And then at Beechwood High I met a few other girls who were Christians and we started our prayer group.

It seemed natural that I should lead the group. I like leading and the others don't. That worked out fine. It was all good training for what would come later.

Rod had said to me at the club one evening, "You know, Willow, don't you, that God has a plan for your life?"

This was news to me. I said, "What do you mean?"

"Well," he said, "Whenever anyone decides to invite God into their lives, he takes them at their word. He comes in, and takes control. He has a plan for each one of our lives, just waiting for us to be willing to fit into it."

I found this idea exciting, astonishing and just a little scary. What if God wanted me to do something I really hated, like teaching Maths – or teaching anything, for that matter? Rod saw the expression on my face and laughed. "Don't worry, Willow! God doesn't usually require us to do something we're not fitted for. He's the one who gives us our gifts and our talents and we're all different. He wants us to be happy and fulfilled in our work for him. He'll reveal what he wants you to do, and it might be through the things you're most passionate about."

I went home thinking this over, feeling a new excitement inside me. God was going to do something with my life. I felt the future stretch ahead, full of thrilling prospects.

I suppose that, in spite of myself, I've inherited something from Mum and Dad, because I'm quite artistic too. I've always been interested in graphics and design, especially textiles and fashion. Maybe it's because I had to wear such dire clothes as a child; long droopy hippie skirts and clumpy boots and baggy jumpers that Mum knitted herself. Maybe I'm still rebelling after all, because when a couple of years ago I was given quite a big sum of money by an aunt to buy clothes (I think she felt sorry for me and the way I had to dress), I knew exactly what I wanted. No more hippie gear. No more Goth or weird stuff. What I headed for was the cool gear, the elegant jeans that looked so good on my long slim legs, the Diesel sportswear and designer label tops and jackets. I bought one or two good things that day, and have stuck to my guns since. I don't wear High Street stuff any more. It's Grace Ellen and Dior for me.

I reckon I might be a designer myself one day. Another Stella McCartney, only better. Maybe the world's first leading Christian fashion designer. God can use all our talents, and with God all things are possible.

And I aim to begin now by looking the part.

## *two*

Because of our little brothers being friends, Annie and I were soon in and out of each other's houses a lot. I would have to go and pick up Rowan from hers, or she would come to mine to fetch Harry.

The second time she came round, I asked her up into my bedroom, where hopefully we'd get some peace and quiet. Dad was home doing some research on the Internet, and Mum had a commission for a painting, which meant she stuck at it day and night and couldn't think of anything else. The house was a mess, canvases stacked in the sitting room to give her space to work in her little studio, cushions and papers littered about, the kitchen full of piled-up pots and pans waiting for someone to wash them. We traipsed up the un-vacuumed stairs, avoiding piles of books and clothing parked on the steps, and opened the door to my room.

I saw Annie's eyes open wide in surprise. She said, "Oh! This is lovely."

I was pretty pleased with my bedroom. I'd got some really nice fine gauzy material, metres of it, from the Oxfam shop, blue with a kind of subtle silver thread running through it, and made a bedspread with matching curtains and wall hangings. There was a desk and a whole row of plain wardrobes, which I'd painted and added brushed metal handles and knobs. I had a big blue suede floor cushion and an Anglepoise desk lamp with a silver shade, and a white faux fur throw on the bed. It all came together with a subtle, classy kind of effect. And I always kept it as neat as a pin.

She wandered around, admiring the details, looking at the paintings on the walls. One of them is me as a child, with my hair all fanned out round my head like a flame. Needless to say, it's one of Mum's.

I couldn't believe the difference in Annie. She didn't

seem the same person as the scared, rabbity kind of girl who'd scuttled round with her head down and her hair half-covering her face. Now she stood up straight and looked you in the eye. She could hold a proper conversation and liked a laugh. She was fitting in well with the rest of the gang.

I said, "Yes, it is pretty cool. I spend a lot of time up here. Want to have a look at my gear?"

I flung open one of the wardrobe doors and saw Annie's eyes go wide again as she looked inside. I keep everything in perfect order, jeans and trousers in one section, tops in another, jumpers folded on the shelves, jackets all together, shoes and boots lined up on racks, hats, gloves, scarves and belts all in their own compartments. And all colour co-ordinated, so I can see at a glance what will go with what outfit.

Annie said, "Wow! What fantastic stuff!"

"Have a closer look if you like," I said, and she did, pulling out a top here, a jacket there, looking at the labels, stroking the material of some suede trousers. Then she repeated, "Wow! It's like some designer boutique all of your own. Such stacks of things! Your parents must be loaded."

Then she stopped and blushed, let her hair fall forward and looked like she had that first day at school, scared she'd said something out of place.

I laughed and said, "No, they're not. Half the time, they haven't got two pennies to rub together. They're not all that good with money. Especially Mum. She spends like crazy when she's just sold a painting or something, then it's back to baked beans and pasta. No, I use my own money. Save everything I get for birthdays and Christmases – I've got one aunt who's really well off. But I earn the rest."

"What do you do to earn money?" She looked puzzled. I guessed she'd never had to worry too much about money.

"Do jobs. I baby-sit. I sometimes do washing-up at a restaurant in the evenings. I walk people's dogs for them. Do shopping for old people. Help with a holiday playgroup. Lots of things."

I could see she was well impressed. "And all the money you earn goes on clothes?"

"Most of it. Designer ones, though. I don't like the usual High Street stuff. It's tacky. I'm into Grace Ellen just now. Their knitwear is just brill."

I pulled out the latest one from its place, a little mint-green cardigan with ruffle cuffs. I hadn't worn it yet. But I loved the shape of it, the look and feel of the soft cashmere. I held it out to Annie. "Try it on." She did. She's a bit smaller than me, but even so it looked good on her. I sighed with satisfaction. "You can't beat GE."

Annie admired herself in my long mirror with the wavy edges. Then she took the cardigan off and carefully hung it up again on its hanger, making sure the shoulders were fitted properly. I liked that. I don't like to see clothes thrown down in a heap or crumpled up.

She was looking at me all admiringly. "You could be a model if you wanted to. Is that what you're going to be?"

I'd thought about modelling. I knew I had the figure for it, tall and skinny like Mum, and the kind of red hair and green eyes and pale skin that stands out. But I wasn't quite sure that modelling was me, especially since I'd become a Christian.

"What I really want is to be a designer," I said. "Study Art and Design first, of course. Then go into business creating really quality stuff. Like this," I waved my hand at the rails of clothes in my wardrobe, "only better. I want to be the best designer ever. The best Christian designer."

She looked mystified. "What does that mean?"

I wasn't quite sure myself. But I knew that I had certain gifts, given to me by God. Rod and Sadie had told me that I could be a witness to God's love wherever I was. I knew I loved clothes, I loved textiles, I loved the cut and hang and style of designer gear. I also knew that the fashion industry might be a very hard one to get into, and very difficult to stand up for what I believed while being part of it. But I was strong. I was sure I could do it.

# *three*

The Beech Bank Club is a bit of a miracle itself, in my opinion. Rod became vicar at St John's five or six years ago, and right away he and Sadie noticed that there weren't any proper youth club facilities in the town. They also noticed that a lot of people – including several of their congregation – were always moaning about the young people of the town hanging about the car park, whizzing round the pavements on skateboards, playing in the streets, making lots of noise, etc, etc. St John's hall didn't offer much hope – it's quite small with only one room and a tiny kitchen, all right for church socials and old people's teas, but not much good for anyone under about fifty-five!

Then they found that the local authority Community Centre was in fact not much used for the community, except for Beavers, Darby & Joan and a "Youth Night" that didn't offer much more than table tennis and pool, and was so uncool that hardly anyone ever went to it. The place was also tatty and in bad repair, the Council being short of funds.

Rod talked to the Council and didn't get far. So he and Sadie prayed. Then they talked again. The Council said that they'd let them use the place, but the rent they suggested was huge. Rod and Sadie and others prayed some more. Then someone had the idea of offering to repair and redecorate the place in exchange for an affordable rent. Bingo! The Council jumped at it, and Rod organised some of the young people, who got busy with tools and paint and lots of enthusiasm.

Result: a whole building, all spick and span, with kitchen facilities, café area, snooker, pool, TV, computers – even an indoor sports hall – that's open five afternoons a week, starting at 4pm so that people can go there right after school for an hour or two if they want, and go back later in the evening. Rod or Sadie or some of their helpers are on hand and there's always someone to talk to if you need it. There's even a Quiet Room for homework. It's ace! I don't know how I'd get along without the Beech Bank Club now.

We all went down there again on the Friday after Annie had first come to the club. Fridays are the most popular, with no school next day. The first person we met was Sadie, all in a fluster with the two kids in tow. Baby Abi was grizzling, and Josh was hanging onto his mother's trouser leg and looking sorry for himself. Sadie seemed very glad to see us, especially me.

She said, "I'm in a flat spin this afternoon. Rod's away conducting a funeral, my baby sitter's let me down, Abi's teething and Josh is going down with something – I'm popping him down to the surgery now. I've opened up the club, and Hugh is here to keep an eye on things." (Hugh is a helper who mostly does sports with the boys.) "But there's the Enquirer's class this afternoon. I normally lead that, as you know." She looked at me with real appeal in her brown eyes. "Willow, you're a committed Christian and I know you're a good leader. Do you think you could, just this once, take the class for me? It's just a matter of following this week's session in the course book, really, and then a discussion afterwards. You'll remember from when you did it. There are four or five girls coming at the moment. What do you think?"

I was a bit gobsmacked, to say the least, but I could see she was really in a spot. I'd been a Christian for over a year, and I'd learned quite a bit. As she'd said, I liked to lead. I was strong. I felt I could do it.

"Well, okay then. Yes, I'll give it a go. You get off and don't worry."

She thanked me from the heart, and we helped her strap the two little ones into their car seats and waved them off. I took a deep breath. No sitting about over coffee this afternoon exchanging all the hot goss. I had responsibilities.

"What's an Enquirer's class?" asked Annie as we went back inside.

"It's a kind of group for those who want to know more about Christianity," I explained, heading for the snug. The others drifted off to the café area, but Annie stuck with me. "Can anyone come? Could I?"

I was searching for the Youth Bibles and the work books that we used for the class. "Yes, of course," I said. "Annie, could you help me find the books? I've got the Bibles but I don't know where the course books are."

We were still searching when the girls turned up for the class, three of them, all from Beechwood High but in the year below us. We still had not found the work books, and I couldn't spend any more time looking. I'd have to improvise.

We got everyone sitting down, and I explained the situation.

"We'll – um – start with prayer," I said. I managed the prayer okay, and found a Bible reading I thought would suit, about Jesus never turning away anyone who came to him. Then I was a bit stuck.

"Is there – er – is there anything anyone would like to ask?" I said.

The Year Nines looked at each other. Then one of them said, "I've got a question."

I smiled encouragingly, and she went on, "How can I get my dad to let me have my belly button pierced?"

The other two giggled. Annie looked embarrassed, both for them and for me.

I thought for a moment, and said, "Well, maybe you need to try and see your dad's point of view. Listen to his reasons. Maybe he's worried about infection, that kind of thing. Talk to him. Communicate."

I felt I'd handled it rather well. I cleared my throat,

and went on, "However, what I meant was questions of a spiritual nature."

They quietened down. Then another girl, Molly, piped up. "I'd like to ask if it's true that God knows everybody in the whole world. Like, there are millions and millions. Does he really know every single person?"

I felt on firmer ground here. Rod and Sadie had instructed me well. "Yes, every single one," I said. "And what's more, he loves every one. Unconditionally. That means we don't have to earn his love." I was warming to my subject. "In fact, God knows us so well that he knows exactly how many hairs we have on our heads. Imagine that." I ran my hand over my own unruly red hair. That thought always blew my mind away. How could someone have such knowledge of us, and such love? Yet that's the way it is.

To my surprise, Annie put up her hand. "Willow, can I ask something? Could you tell me please, how people believe in God? I mean, you can't see him, hear him, touch him or anything. How can you tell he's real? How can it be proved?"

She was really curious. I drew another deep breath and said, "It's all about faith. Each of us has faith, that's what the Bible says. Each of us has to use the faith we have. We have to read the Bible. Pray. God will give us faith to believe, if we ask him."

She looked thoughtful. I think I explained it okay.

Someone was asking something else, and I was

answering. I managed to find answers for all the questions that came up and the session went by quite quickly.

I'd managed it. I'd somehow had the words to say, without the books, and even Annie was interested. I felt well chuffed. Sadie would be pleased.

# *four*

Next day, Saturday, we had decided to go shopping. Chloe was away visiting her brother in hospital – he has some illness that means he's sometimes in hospital. It seemed the ideal time to get some stuff together for her surprise party. The rest of us – Rachel, Amber, Holly, Annie and me – took the bus to the city twenty miles away.

We were all in a good mood. I was still on a bit of a high after the night before at the Beech Bank Club. We'd called at the vicarage on the way to catch the bus, and Sadie and Rod were pleased too. Little Josh had an ear infection but was already feeling better after starting on an antibiotic. Sadie was so grateful I'd stepped in to help, and managed even without the workbooks, which she'd later found under the nappy bag on the back seat of her car. I felt a warm glow inside.

Some of the sixth formers from Beechwood High were on the bus, including Mark Westlake, the school soccer captain, and some of his mates. Mark is a seriously fit guy, and Holly has daydreamed about him for ages. As it happened, I shared a seat with Amber, and Rachel with Annie. That left Holly sitting on her own, until – guess who came and sat down beside her? Her face went pink and she came over all coy and silly. The rest of us shook our heads and rolled up our eyes, but maybe we were only jealous. As I said, Mark is definitely a cool dude.

Anyway, Holly got over the shock and soon the two of them seemed to be hitting it off, chatting away, heads together, all through the journey. When we reached the city and got off, Holly seemed quite sorry that Mark and his mates were going off one way and the rest of us another.

"Guess what!" she said, as we headed towards the precinct. "He's only asked me out next weekend! I can't wait! Isn't he amazing?"

Her face was all glowing and her eyes sparkling. The others all told her that she was one jammy customer. I felt a little twinge of unease.

"Is he a Christian, Holls?"

"No," said Holly, "At least, I don't think so. Why?"

"Well," I said, "*You* are, and you know we're not supposed to hitch up with people who aren't."

Some of the sparkle left her face. Her eyebrows drew together in a frown. "Oh, for goodness' sake,

Willow! I'm not planning to *marry* him! I know the score. It's just a date, for goodness' sake! What's your problem?"

She stalked on ahead, all huffy. I didn't want to upset her and spoil the day for all of us. But I knew what the Bible says about close friendships with unbelievers. I felt I'd done right in saying something. Hadn't I?

I caught up with her and touched her arm. "Sorry, Holls, I didn't mean to go on. I just don't want you making mistakes."

"Yeah, right. But just remember, Willow, I do have a mind of my own. I don't need to ask your permission, even if you are a leader and all that."

"Okay. Friends?" I said, and she unbent and said, "Friends." And we both stuck out our little fingers and linked them together. All the others breathed a sigh of relief, and we hit the shops big time.

Our first call was at one of those party places where they sell everything festive you can think of – balloons, banners, cards, candles, party bags etc, etc. We'd decided we were going to decorate the club with loads and loads of balloons, silver and red. We had a slight disagreement about the balloons – Amber and Rachel wanted to get about 3,000 gas-filled balloons, until the rest of us pointed out that we'd have difficulty getting them onto the bus. And if we did, the bus would probably rise into the air with all that gas on board. In the end we compromised, and got six big silver gas-filled balloons, and loads of the ones you blow up (red) plus a balloon pump. We got one huge balloon with Happy Birthday on it and a big banner with the same. Then we chose silver candles to contrast with the red-checked tablecloths, party poppers (the kind that shoot out paper streamers), wrapping paper, cards and some music to put us in a party mood.

By then we thought it was time for lunch, so went to the local McDonalds, Rachel hanging on to the bunch of big silver balloons and the rest of us clutching bags. All of us were pals again now. Holly and I had forgotten our differences, there was a great atmosphere and we had a lot of laughs.

Afterwards, we tackled the serious present buying. We discussed at length Chloe's favourite things, and in the end Holly and Amber bought a black top and a white one respectively, Rachel got a chunky bracelet, I got a pendant to match, and Annie, on our advice, picked a DVD by Chloe's favourite group. All of us got books and chocs.

That left us with still a couple of hours to spare before the bus home. Time to check out the clothes shops, see what's new, maybe treat ourselves (we'd been saving like mad for this trip). So we headed for the High Street, balloons and all.

Being Saturday, the shops were packed with people our age, chattering, laughing, rifling through the racks of clothes, running back and forth to the changing rooms with hangers full of gear to try on. All the others love that scene and dived right in. I find it all a bit tacky – all that stuff looks the same and some of it isn't too well made. Often the finish isn't good and the seams begin to fall apart after a few wearings. I rubbed the fabric of a denim skirt between my fingers – very thin and poor quality. Nothing I'd want here. So I opted to be balloon minder and stood out of the way near the door while the others ran in and out of the changing rooms. We moved from shop to shop and all of them bought something. Holly got a pair of combats and a crop top – you can bet those were for her big date with Mark. Rachel and Amber both got T-shirts and Annie bought a leather belt with a big silver buckle.

Rachel took the balloons to give my hand a rest. "Anywhere you fancy going, Wills?"

There was somewhere I liked, and we still had time to go there. A huge, exclusive department store, Chadwick's, at the posh end of the shopping centre. It had everything, classy household stuff, sleek expensive furniture, classic ladies' wear, trendy children's clothes that cost a fortune. And – a teen department, full of designer labels.

"Let's go to Chadwick's," I said.

# *five*

We were all laughing and chattering as we went in through the revolving doors at Chadwick's, but we fell silent as one by one we got inside. Chadwick's has that kind of effect on you. The carpets are the sort that you sink in up to your ankles and the atmosphere is hushed and almost reverent.

The assistants wear elegant cream suits, their hair is immaculate, their nails long and polished, and they hover discreetly as you look at the goods. Even in the Teen Wear department, which we made a beeline for, it's the same, except that the stuff they sell is bang up-to-the-minute.

I just love the whole atmosphere, but the others were a little nervous.

"I'd never dare try anything on here," said Amber in a whisper, as we approached a dummy in black suede jeans, a silk top, pale blue fur jacket and black suede boots with long pointy toes.

"Why ever not?" I asked. I'd bought a lot of my stuff here, most of it costing a fortune, all hard-earned by me. We wandered round, looking at the racks of jeans, dresses, skirts, jackets and everything else imaginable.

"There's nothing to stop you trying clothes on if you want to," I said. "Let's dump this stuff and check out a few things."

So, under the cool gaze of the blonde assistant, we made a huge pile of our High Street bags, with the silver balloons tied on top. A couple of us sat on the elegant gilt chairs while the others chose what they wanted to try and took them to the cream-curtained cubicles. I was getting the adrenalin rush I always have when I'm around well-designed clothes.

Rachel tried on a lilac flowery dress, which didn't suit her at all, and then a little canvas skirt and waistcoat, which did. Amber looked incredibly cool in pink hipsters and matching top, and Holly wished she'd waited and got her combats here, as these ones made her High Street ones look cheap. They were getting the hang of it now, despite the rather disapproving looks we were getting from the blonde assistant. In and out of the cubicles they went, taking care to replace each article of clothing on the hangers afterwards. Each time the assistant drew near and enquired whether she could help, the girls replied that no, thank you, they were just looking.

Annie was the only one who actually bought anything. She said that her dad had sent her some money (he seems to be something big in IT) but she wasn't that keen on spending it. She seemed quite hurt still about the break-up. But we did persuade her to buy a baby-blue top which looked good. She went back afterwards to try on a matching mini-skirt, but decided against it.

Then it was my turn. I picked out a pair of trousers I'd had my eye on from the start, GE, chocolate brown (my favourite colour just now), sleek and classy. They fitted me perfectly. My legs seemed to go on for ever as I looked at myself from all angles in the triple mirrors. The floor was carpeted in cream to match the thick cream curtains, the mirrors were outlined in gilt. Soft seductive music played, to put customers into a buying mood. I loved the whole ambience of the place.

And I wanted those trousers. I wanted them badly. I sighed. The price tag was seventy pounds. I had nowhere near that much left, probably no more than a tenner. But if only! I looked at myself again, from the front, back, sides, bending, stretching, with my heels on and without. They looked gorgeous from every angle, as though they'd been made just for me. I didn't need trousers, I had a whole rail full at home. But these were something to die for.

It was no good. I sighed again, unzipped the trousers and began to climb out of them. Then suddenly I noticed something, half concealed by the jeans and bag I'd dumped on the chair. A purse. It wasn't mine, but I thought I knew who it belonged to. I was sure I'd seen this one, or one just like it, clutched in Annie's hand. And Annie had used this cubicle just before me.

To make sure, I picked it up and opened it. Yes,

there was her name on a label in a clear plastic window inside.

Then, suddenly, I found myself unzipping the cash compartment. I felt my eyes widen. A whole roll of notes was there – and none of them were under twenty-pound ones. There must be about three hundred pounds in cash, at least. She'd said that her dad had given her money but I'd no idea it was this much.

I don't quite know what happened next. But almost before I knew it, I'd peeled off three of the twenty-pound notes. With those I could buy the trousers. It was only a loan. Annie might not even miss them. I'd pay her back when I'd earned some money.

And then I came to my senses and realised what I had been contemplating. Heart thudding, I replaced the money and zipped up the purse. All of a sudden I felt sick to my stomach. What on earth had happened to me in those split seconds? I'd almost stolen money, I was no better than a common thief. The shame of it almost made me dizzy.

Then the dizziness receded, and I could hear the soft buzz of the girls' voices talking outside. One of them called out, "Willow? How're you doing? Come out and give us a twirl."

Still half-dressed, I took the purse and stuck out my hand with it between the curtains. "You left your purse, Annie."

She took it and thanked me. Shaking, I got dressed,

drew the curtain and took the chocolate trousers back
to the rail. I couldn't believe what had almost happened
in there. Here I was, a Christian, a leader, someone
the others looked up to. I'd led an enquiry group the
afternoon before. Just today I'd been lecturing Holly
on the dangers of doubtful relationships. And then
this happened, all because I fancied some trousers
with a designer label.

I couldn't wait to get out of Chadwick's. We
trooped across to the lift with our bags and balloons.
Rachel asked me if I was okay and Amber said I
looked a bit pale. I began to tell them I was fine, but
then something inside me seemed to say that I must
confess. I had to tell them what had happened, or
almost happened.

I said I had something to say, and we all went to
a grassy area with seats not far from the bus station.
They were all looking at me oddly, wondering what
was coming. I took a deep breath and told them.

I didn't quite know how they'd react. Holly in
particular might have every right to crow over me.
And Annie would be hurt. All of them would probably
be well disappointed and disgusted with me.

But they weren't. The apology was scarcely off my
lips before Annie was giving me a hug and saying, "It's
okay, Willow. Partly my fault for being so careless.
Shouldn't have been carrying all that amount anyway
– Mum did warn me. And you didn't take anything."

"But I *wanted* to. Just for a moment."

"But you *didn't*! And Willow, if you really want those trousers, I'll *lend* you the money!"

Tears came into my eyes. But I no longer wanted the trousers at all. I gave her hand a squeeze. She's a friend in a million. They all are.

"Doesn't Rod always say it's not being tempted that's wrong, it's giving in to it?" said Amber. She gave me a hug too, and then the others all joined in a big soppy group hug. Then we went for a quick coffee at Starbucks before the bus came in.

I felt better, but still shaken. How could I let something like a designer fashion item bring me to this point? To actually consider committing a crime, and, worse, to let down my best and closest friends. I thought long and hard about priorities, travelling home on the bus. I realised God had kept me safe at my time of weakness. I'd always considered myself a strong person, but I saw now that when push comes to shove it's *his* strength we need to get us through. He hadn't let me down though, because I belong to him. Whatever else might happen in my life, I'm very clearly marked with his designer label.

# PART THREE

# Rachel's Story

## ONE STEP TOO MANY

# one

I've known Willow for years, ever since we were bestest friends at primary school, and I've always looked up to her. She seemed to me to be everything a person should be – stunning looking, smart, confident, strong, a born leader. And, since she became a Christian, someone with a strong faith. It was partly through her influence that I became a Christian myself.

We were all a bit gobsmacked when she confessed to us that she'd almost nicked money from Annie's purse in that posh store. At first I couldn't believe it. I mean, *I* might have been tempted like that myself, but I'd never have believed it of her. And I'm dead sure I'd never have admitted it to the others.

For a moment I wondered whether I could ever feel the same respect for Willow when she confessed what nearly happened. Only for a moment though. Because I saw how much courage it must have taken to make the confession, how much easier just to say nothing. We'd never have known. And I've ended up respecting her more than ever.

That day is one that stands out in my memory for other reasons. I got off the bus first, because I live at the other end of town from the others, almost out in the country in fact, in a big old house that used to be a farmhouse. The town has gradually crept up on it over the years as new buildings have gone up, but there are still fields and trees to look out on from our windows. It's approached by a winding drive, which I trudged up after getting off the bus. I'd been appointed balloon-minder, and the silver balloons floated up above my head. I was going to anchor them in the garden shed until they were needed for the party.

I knew something was different the moment I got through the door. Bags were parked in the hall, and voices came from the sitting room, more voices than our usual family of Mum, my stepfather, my sister Ruth and me.

Then the door opened and Ruth came out. She's just two years younger than me, but at that moment she looked a lot younger than twelve, with a sullen expression and gritted teeth. She saw me, stopped, and said dramatically, "Well, that's it! My life is ruined!"

Ruth always tends to make a big deal of everything, she's a drama queen, just like Amber. This time though she looked really cheesed off.

I said, "What's up, then?"

"Only the invasion of the monster step-siblings!" she said bitterly. "They've moved in, haven't they, the whole bunch of them."

"You don't mean . . ." I put down my bags with a horrid sinking feeling.

"I do mean. All of them – Maxwell included. Their mother's gone into hospital or something, suddenly. And they're all here. To stay. Indefinitely. It's – it's – it's – *pants*!"

Her lip wobbled and she looked near to tears. I felt my own heart sink into my shoes. "That means you and I will have to share a room," I said slowly. She nodded, burst into tears and ran sobbing up the stairs, closing her bedroom door with a slam.

I'd come in feeling great, and now my bubble had well and truly burst. Of course, we knew our step-siblings quite well. Too well. They lived with their mother about fifty miles away, but every few weeks came to stay with their father – Ted, our stepdad – for the weekend. Occasionally he went down there to visit, taking Mum along. Once or twice we'd all gone away together. It was never exactly a failure but never exactly a success either. Mostly, we managed to endure it.

Actually, they weren't bad kids, most of them. Billie, the youngest, was rather cute, a little gappy-toothed seven year old who tagged about after me and Ruth and liked trying on party dresses and playing with Barbie dolls. We could cope with her all right. There were twins of ten, a girl and a boy, Jade and Benjamin. They were bearable as well, in small doses, if only they hadn't been forever scrapping. Ruth and I had the odd falling-out and were quite capable of screeching like fishwives on occasions. But Jade and Ben continually bickered, fought, argued, wrangled and generally were a pain in the neck. Ted gave them a lot of leeway but sometimes came down hard on them. Mum said they'd probably grow out of it. Mum tries to be optimistic. Ruth and I often felt like banging their heads together.

But Maxwell was the one who really got up our noses. Maxwell came between Ruth and me in age. At thirteen he was small for his age, a bit spotty, floppy fair hair, round eyes behind glasses. A bit of a geek. He was reckoned to be extremely bright, but in our opinion that was very overrated. His voice was beginning to change and sometimes went off into a squeak, which made him blush. But mostly he had a superior way with him, as though we were inferior beings or something.

I was remembering all these negative traits when the sitting room door opened again and Mum came out. She looked harassed and no wonder. "Oh, Rachel, there you are. Has Ruth told you what's happened?"

I nodded, feeling my mouth go down even further at the corners. She looked at me appealingly. "You will try to be nice, won't you? It may not be for too long. Their mother was rushed into hospital, had to have emergency surgery. Don't quite know how serious it is, but she'll need time to convalesce. We'll manage all right if we all pull together."

Who was she trying to convince, herself or me?

Having Maxwell about does not bring out the best in me. But I sighed and said "I'll try, Mum."

She looked relieved. "It'll mean you and Ruth sharing, I'm afraid, for the duration. Max and Ben will need her room. Billie and Jade will be in the spare. I've sent Ruth up to move whatever she wants from her room into yours."

From the thumpings and bangings and muttered exclamations from my sister's room, I gathered she was doing so with a very bad grace. As I trudged upstairs, she emerged with a huge armful of clothes, cuddly toys, duvets and pillows that she carried across and flung onto the floor of my room. Then she went back for another. I looked helplessly at the muddle in the middle of the floor.

Ruth was bringing in the third load when there were steps on the stairs and Maxwell himself was coming up carrying a bag. He stopped at our door and blinked at us from behind his owl spectacles. He'd grown a bit since last time and was about my height now, which isn't very tall. But even so, he managed to give the impression of looking down at us as though we were a bad smell under his nose.

"Oh, hello, Max*well*," I said. He likes to be called Max, so we always make a point of accentuating the *well*.

"Hello there," he said in his geeky way. "Sorry about this. About you having to move rooms."

"Oh, please don't mention it," said Ruth sarcastically. "It's no trouble at all. Please don't give it another thought."

The sarcasm was wasted on Maxwell. "That's good of you. Don't worry if the room's not very tidy. As long as I've got somewhere for my laptop."

He went into Ruth's room and put down his bag, looking round at the tip Ruth had left. Ruth and I exchanged glances behind his back. What a complete nerd! The thought came to me that we weren't being exactly kind to someone whose mother was ill, but I shrugged it off. If we had to put up with geeky Maxwell for an indefinite time, then he would have to put up with us.

# two

It was chaotic at home for a few days, with everyone getting themselves sorted out and settling in. Mum and Ted went around looking permanently hassled, and I was not surprised. They'd been able to get the three younger ones, Ben, Jade and Billie, into the local primary school for the duration of their stay. For one horrible moment I thought Maxwell might have to come to our school. Imagine what that would do to my street cred! But it was decided that he would study at home, working on projects set for him by his old school.

The Monday after they'd arrived, Ruth and I got

home from school to find all the others home and the house bursting at the seams. Billie was prancing around in a pink tutu with sequins, bare feet and her hair done up in bunches, repeating over and over, "I'm a ballerina princess! I'm a ballerina princess!" She spun round in front of Ruth and me and said it again. "Look at me! I'm a ballerina princess!"

"Yeah, yeah, very nice," I said grumpily. After a day in school I'm in no mood for kiddie games. I just want a cup of tea and a bit of quiet. No chance here.

Ruth is often nicer than me, so she spent a bit of time admiring Billie's tutu and asking her to do a twirl and show her some ballet steps. Ben and Jade were supposed to be doing homework upstairs, but were bickering between themselves as usual.

I sighed, remembering life as it used to be.

My dad died five years ago when I was nine and Ruth was seven. I can remember him well, although I don't think about him much. He was medium height with broad shoulders, dark hair and dark eyes. Mum says I'm like him to look at. I remember the cuddles we had, Ruth and I, sitting with Dad in a big blue armchair, one on each side, listening to him read *Winnie-the-Pooh* and *The Wind in the Willows*, feeling warm and safe and loved. I remember the way we sometimes got out of bed, when he was late home from work, and rushed down the stairs in our nighties to hug him.

"Little princesses in pretty nightdresses," he used to

call us. I remember Ruth and me running on a sunlit beach, away from Mum and Dad, and looking back to see them holding hands as they strolled after us.

Those were the safe years. The anxious uncertain ones came later, when Dad was ill and gave up work, and was sometimes at home and sometimes in hospital, and didn't run with us any more and after a while didn't even pick us up and cuddle us. Then he was gone, and Mum seemed gone too, leaving a pale ghost of herself in her place, quiet and sad.

Ruth cried a lot but I didn't. I tried my best to pretend that nothing had happened. That I didn't remember those good times. That I'd never had a dad, even. And that I didn't care anyway.

Time passed, and gradually good times came again. Mum and Ruth and I were a tight little group, sticking together, eating together, shopping together. Sometimes when one of us was a bit lonely we even all slept together in the big king-sized bed.

And then, one day, there was Ted. Mum met him through her part-time secretarial job. The first time she brought him home to meet us I could see there was a change in her. Instead of the pale quiet woman, suddenly she was like a girl again, eyes soft and shiny, cheeks glowing. She had her hair done a new way and bought some new clothes.

Ted was a tall man, grey at the temples, with hazel eyes behind spectacles because he was short-sighted. He was a bit vague, kind, mild-mannered, clever and very good at his job. Ruth and I didn't know what to make of him at first. We resented him intruding into our lives, and half-planned to make his life a misery and play all kinds of tricks on him, like putting salt in his tea instead of sugar. But something stopped us. For one thing, he made our mum happy and sparkly again. For another, he was a nice man.

His kids were the real shock to the system. By the time Mum and Ted got married, we'd got to know each other, sort of. Their mother had gone off with someone else, and she and Ted were divorced long before Mum came on the scene. But at first they sometimes acted as though Mum was a wicked stepmother or something, which made us mad. But we'd got over that phase now. By the time we'd moved to this bigger house, we'd all got used to the situation, more or less.

"Hello! Earth to Rachel! Come in please!"

I jumped, realising I was still standing in the hallway and that Mum was speaking to me, waving a hand in front of my face.

"Oh. Hello, Mum."

"You were miles away. In this racket, too." She sighed, and called up the stairs. "Ben! Jade! Calm down, for goodness' sake. Your dad will be home soon. Billie, you'd better take that off before it gets ripped, darling. Ruth, help her, would you?"

She sighed. I realised how hard it must be for her, having four extra children dumped on her at a moment's notice.

"Thank goodness they're at school all day," she said. "Except for Max, of course."

"Poor you," I said. "Having geeky Maxwell in the house all day long."

She gave me quite a sharp look. "Don't be horrid. Max is no trouble at all. He gets on with his work. And he's helpful too. He fetched wood and coal in for me today, took out the rubbish and even peeled the potatoes for dinner."

Trust Maxwell, the creep, trying to worm his way into Mum's good books and show up the rest of us.

Mum went on, "It's him I wanted to talk to you about, actually. I think it's going to be dreadfully dull and boring for Max, just being here in the house on his own all day. I'm here, of course, but he needs to be meeting other young people. I was wondering – well, it's just an idea, but I thought maybe you'd take him along with you to the Beech Bank Club one of these afternoons."

I stared at her, aghast! What, go to the club with geeky Maxwell in tow, all specs and spots and nerdy comments?

"Maybe he won't fancy it," Mum went on. "But I think it would be nice at least to ask, don't you think?"

I wanted to scream, almost. The club is *my* place, *my* refuge, where I meet *my* friends, hang out with *my* mates, talk over *my* concerns and share *my* thoughts. Ruth goes now and again now she's twelve, and that's cool. But I don't want Maxwell there. I do not. No. Never.

Mum was almost pleading with me. "Think about it, Rachel, please."

I nodded and picked up my bag to go upstairs. But inside I was repeating, over and over, "Sorry Mum, it can't be done. No way."

# *three*

Well, I took him to Beech Bank. Not willingly, not gladly, not welcomingly (if there is such a word). Grudgingly, resentfully, and feeling well embarrassed.

Everyone there was nice to him, but then they're always nice to everybody. The girls rushed up and Amber said, "So this is your brother, Rach."

I gave her a look, and said, "My *step*brother, actually."

Anyway, they took him off and introduced him to some of the lads, and after a while I saw him playing pool with a couple of them, peering short-sightedly along the cue. He seemed to be enjoying himself too. I sighed. I suppose that meant he'd be tagging along with me all the time, given half a chance.

Sadie came over and sat down opposite with a coffee. "All right, Rachel? You look a bit down in the dumps."

I straightened up my shoulders and looked at her

smiley brown eyes. Sadie is always a good person to talk to. Before I realised it, I was sounding off about the situation at home, all those kids dumped upon us and a nerd like Maxwell dogging my footsteps. She looked thoughtful, stirring her coffee. Then she said, "You know, Rachel, this doesn't sound a bit like you. You're usually the first there if anyone needs a bit of help. You and the rest have been so good with Annie, for instance."

"Yes, but that's different," I said. "Annie needed help. She's had such a rough time. Besides, she's great. Not all superior and geeky like *him*."

I realised I sounded a bit like a sulky ten year old, whining and complaining. Sadie smiled a little. "It can't be easy for you all living together. But it can't be easy for Max and the others either, being suddenly uprooted and separated from their mum. And maybe you're misjudging Max. He doesn't come over as superior to me. Just a bit shy."

I hadn't thought of it like that. In fact, I realised with a sense of shame, that I hadn't considered their point of view at all. Or maybe, to be absolutely honest, hadn't wanted to.

"You know the best thing to do with someone you find it difficult to get on with?" she asked. I thought – avoid them? Be extra nice to them? Pretend you like them? But I shook my head.

She said, "Pray for them. If we pray, it invites God to work in the situation. He can change things."

"You mean, he'll change Maxwell?" That was a novel thought. Maxwell, changing into someone charming, cool, fit and hunky, like Clark Kent changing into Superman on those old films. I couldn't help grinning.

Sadie said, "Maybe. Maybe he'll change the circumstances too. And maybe he'll change you."

Me? I'm not the one needing to change, am I? Maxwell's the one with the problems.

But I'd always listened to Sadie before, and something told me I should listen now.

So I said, "Well, okay. I'll try. Thanks, Sadie."

"You're welcome. And I'll pray for you all too." She reached across and patted my shoulder, and then got up and went to talk to someone else.

I actually did feel a bit better, a bit more sympathetic to Maxwell and the other kids. I made up my mind I would pray, and I'd try to be nicer too.

I almost forgot about Maxwell and had a good goss with the other girls and then a game of table tennis. Chloe and Amber went home early, so the rest of us had a chance to mosey round the café area deciding where we were going to put up the decorations and fix up the tables and so on. We were discussing food with Sadie when I heard Maxwell's voice behind me.

"Rachel, do you think we'd better be getting home? I've got some work to do and you must have homework too. And won't your mum have the meal ready?"

He was looking at me in his usual way, superior as

anything. I thought – what a geek! Then I felt Sadie's eye upon me. So I said, "Oh, is that the time? Maybe we'd better get going."

Amber, Annie, Willow and I usually walked home together. We did now, with Maxwell tagging uncomfortably along. The others tried to include him in the conversation but it was hard going. And then they'd dropped off at their houses, one by one, and it was just him and me, walking up the bumpy drive to our farmhouse.

Well, I couldn't think of one thing to say to him, so I didn't. He trudged along, hands in pockets, eyes fixed on the ground. I wondered if he'd enjoyed the club but couldn't bring myself to ask. Truth to tell, I just wanted to get home and crash out in my room and forget him. Even that wasn't as inviting as it used to be, because Ruth was there half the time, talking on the phone to her mates, listening to music (her tastes aren't mine) or just *being* there, taking up my private space. Everything was difficult.

And then, just as we reached the door, it opened and Billie came charging out, howling like a banshee, and flung herself on Maxwell. "Max! Max! Dad told me off!"

Give him his due, Maxwell is usually nice to his younger siblings. He said, "Shush, Billie. Don't cry. What's it all about?" and gave her a cuddle.

She hiccupped a bit and then said, "It was the balloons. I went in the shed and there were all these lovely silvery balloons, like fairyland, up on the ceiling. So I got a chair and pulled them down – I wanted to see if I would float up in the air and be a magic fairy princess. But then – one got away, and then another." She sobbed and hiccupped. "And then they'd all gone, flying up into the sky. And Dad told me I was very naughty indeed to touch them." She burst into a fresh round of sobs and howls.

Well, wonderful! All our beautiful party balloons I'd brought home and put away so carefully. All gone. And this kid bawling and Maxwell looking at me as though it was all my fault. He did say, "Sorry, Rachel." I was going to say bitterly, "Oh, don't give it another thought!" But just then Billie stopped howling and began to whimper, "I want Mummy!" and as Maxwell bent to hug her again I thought I saw the glint of tears in his eyes too.

So I said nothing and stalked into the house.

## *four*

To give him his due, Ted did apologise too, and offered the money to buy new balloons. I was going to refuse, huffily, but something in his hazel eyes, a lost and sad look, stopped me. So I took the money and thanked him, although he did spoil it a bit by pointing out that

we needed to get the balloons just before the party
date, as they'd start deflating in a couple of days. He'd
actually given us three times as much money as we
needed, so we could get lots more than at first. Later,
I saw him and Mum quickly touch hands, as though
for comfort, when they thought no one was looking. It
was a hard time for them, too.

Things were changing around our house. For one
thing, Ruth and Jade had suddenly become all palsy-
walsy. Ruth and I had always stuck together, shared
our secrets and been best mates out of school. Now,
suddenly, she was spending time with Jade, painting
each other's nails, giggling and looking as though they
had secrets. I was hurt, and tackled Ruth about it a
couple of nights later when we were in bed and the
lights were out.

"What's all this with Jade, then? I thought it was
you and me who were the sisters round here. You and
her never seem to be apart these days."

Ruth seemed surprised. "I like her, that's all. She's
growing up a lot. Haven't you noticed? Ben's still a bit
of a kid but Jade seems older somehow."

I had noticed that Jade was racing ahead of Ben
in many ways. Mum always says that girls grow up
quicker than boys.

"Anyway," Ruth went on. "It's quite nice to be the
older sister for a change, and get to boss someone else
around."

"I don't boss you around!" I said indignantly.

"Yeah, right, if you say so," she said and gave a big yawn. "I'm going to sleep now. Goodnight."

And she was away. Ruth could sleep on a clothesline and nothing ever keeps her awake.

I couldn't sleep though. I put my light on again and lay staring at the ceiling. I felt horrid inside, jealous and resentful, anxious and all churned up. Everything seemed spoiled and all because the Steps were here.

Then I remembered what Sadie had said to me. I picked up my Youth Bible from the bedside table. Sadie and Rod give one of those to each of us who has made the decision to follow Jesus. They're cool, with special sections marked out for certain problems and situations young people may have. I flicked through it, wondering if there was something to help those with difficult stepfamilies. I couldn't find anything right away, but my eye fell on a verse which said: *Casting all your care upon him, because he cares for you.* That made me think. I so much needed someone to care, someone who understood the way I was feeling, because I often didn't understand it myself. I hadn't prayed as Sadie had suggested, in fact I hadn't really prayed at all for days.

I put down the Bible and whispered, "Dear God, I'm so fed up. It's so hard with all these kids living here. Everything's changing. I feel mean all the time, even when I don't want to be. And I just can't stick Maxwell! Please help me." And then I gritted my teeth and added, "And please help Maxwell and the others too."

After what Sadie said I half-expected to feel a sudden warm fuzzy feeling towards Maxwell. I didn't. But slowly, something else happened – a kind of quiet peace, a knowing that God had heard, that he understood my horrid mixed-up feelings, that he was in control of everything. And then I was fast asleep.

At the weekend, Ted decided that he was going to take all the children to visit their mother. Mum offered to go too, but they decided it might be best to go by themselves. So on Saturday morning we waved them all off.

It was absolute bliss to have the whole house to ourselves, just the three of us. As the saying goes, the silence was deafening. No feet pounding up and down stairs, no quarrels, no demanding children's voices. As Mum said (with feeling), five fewer hungry mouths to feed. No Maxwell.

The house had an airy feel, as though it held all the space in the world. Mum set to work at once, tidying away books, games and toys, and giving the place a good spring-clean. She suggested that Ruth and I had a go at the upstairs.

Most of Ruth's possessions were still in heaps on our bedroom floor. In fact, it was worse than before, because all week she'd stirred things around looking for what she needed for school. She put some loud music on and began stirring again, trying to create some order out of chaos. I left her to it and turned to the other rooms, trailing the vacuum cleaner behind me.

Billie and Jade's room was quite a muddle too, with school things, cuddly toys, Barbie dolls (lots of them) and Billie's sparkly, spangly stuff all over the beds, chests and chairs. I began to pick things up, folding and stacking, piling and hanging, until I found enough carpet to vacuum and enough surfaces to dust. It did look better afterwards, though.

I thought Ben and Maxwell's room would be the worst of all, but to my surprise it was relatively neat and tidy. Someone had put all socks and underwear into the basket, the beds were made, clothes put away and computer stuff neatly lined up on the desk. Maxwell's work, I guessed. I couldn't see Ben doing the clean-up bit.

Out of curiosity, I opened and shut a few of the chest and desk drawers allocated to the boys. Clean socks rolled in pairs, DVDs neatly stacked, school books tidily piled. And a red-bound book that looked like a diary.

I shouldn't have, but I did. Really curious now, I picked up the diary and flicked through the pages. Maxwell's handwriting was neat and precise, well, it would be. There was a lot about the stuff he was doing in school, his computer studies, his exam results. Then, in more recent entries, it suddenly got more personal. *"Mum is ill. All of us are worried. She's going to hospital and we may have to stay at Dad's."* *"We're at*

Dad's. We came today. Pat (Mum) *tries to be nice but I don't think they want us here really. Rachel and Ruth don't anyway. Wish we were at home.*"

"*Billie and Jade were crying today.* (I never knew they'd been crying.) *They want to go home. So do I. R and R are sneery, especially Rachel. I have to try and be nice because of the others, but it's v. hard sometimes.*" . . . "*Today I went to a kind of Christian club with Rachel. Met some nice people there. Mum still very ill. Billie in trouble for losing some balloons. Ruth was nice today but Rachel as sneery as ever.*"

It went on. I closed the diary and put it back in the drawer. I had a sick feeling, a feeling of shame. Despite Sadie's talk, I'd never given much thought to what those kids were feeling. I'd only thought about myself, all along. And I was supposed to be the Christian in the family!

I sat down on Ruth's bed (which was now Maxwell's) with the duster in my hand, feeling as though I was falling apart inside, somehow. I fought desperately against the feeling of wanting to cry because I never cried on principle.

Downstairs, the phone began to ring.

# *five*

Mum came up upstairs to find us, walking slowly, her face as white as a sheet. She'd had bad news.

"Rachel? She saw me sitting on the bed, vacuum at my feet, and came and sat down beside me.

"Mum? What's happened?"

Mum put her hands up to her face. "Ted just called. It's the children's mother. She's much more ill than anyone knew. She's . . . dying. Oh, those poor children! Those poor little mites!"

She covered her face. I knew that she was thinking of that time with our dad, of all she'd gone through then. I put my arm round her, but all the time I was thinking – their mum's going to die. Just like Dad did. And I went all hot and cold, imagining how I'd feel if Mum died too. And wondering how Maxwell and the others must be feeling.

It was strange, but it didn't enter my head at all what would happen to the kids now, or that they might even have to come and live permanently with us. All I could think of was what they must be going through.

I gave Mum a hug, and she said, "Thanks, love, I needed that," and then got up and went to find Ruth.

A funny thing happened then. I felt as though something was breaking loose inside me, something that I'd kept tight and close and coiled-up for a long, long time. I went to the door and turned the key in the lock. And then I lay down on Maxwell's bed and sobbed and sobbed as though I'd never stop. Dad was in my mind, and the fact that I'd never see him again, and that I loved him and needed him, and I wondered how he'd felt and if the suffering had been terrible and if he'd hated to go. I sobbed out all the pain and grief I'd been holding in, years of it, and a strange thing happened, because as it left, a whole lot of other things left too, all the resentment and jealousy and mean feelings I'd had about Maxwell and the others.

And then, strangely, I felt that peace again, the peace I'd felt when I prayed the other night, but stronger, and clearer, the peace that the Bible says is past all understanding.

After a long time I sat up and dried my eyes on the duster. I'd cried so much that I'd left a large wet patch on Maxwell's duvet. Ruth's music had been switched off. Ruth and Mum must have heard me sobbing but they'd wisely left me alone to cry it out. I slid off the bed and unlocked the door. Then I went back to the desk, ripped a sheet of paper from the pad and wrote *"Dear Max, I'm sorry I've been such a pig. I'll try to do better. Rachel."*

Ted and the children came back next day, looking pale and quiet. Maxwell must have read my note but he never said anything. He looked at me a bit differently though, the way you'd look at someone you were beginning to trust. The other kids were quiet for a day or two and then got back to usual, even the bickering. Something wasn't quite the same though, and somehow we all knew it. It took me a while to figure out that it was me who'd changed, and that because of that, the whole eight of us were somehow lighter and more free, even with the terrible sadness.

And it *was* a sad time, because a few days later, the children's mother was dead.

All of us went to the funeral; Mum, Ruth and me too. Somehow we sensed that they needed us all to be there. It was sad, but somehow a triumph too. I don't remember Dad's funeral at all, but at this one I felt a sense of something very like joy when the vicar said the words, "*I am the resurrection and the life. He that believes in me, though he were dead, yet shall he live. And he that believes in me shall never die.*"

I had the strong certainty that this life is not all that there is. And I was so touched when all the children, even Max, came to me for a hug as we walked away from the graveside and got into the cars.

Things are moving on now. Mum opened her heart and her home to all of Ted's children and offered them a permanent place here with us. But in the event, there were grandparents who stepped in and decided to look after them during the school term.

Holidays, and some weekends, they will come to us.

I'm sure there will still be major fights sometimes. But I'm also sure we'll manage to shake down okay and put up with each other. There's even been talk of going camping in the Lake District next summer, all eight of us. We must be mad!

As for Maxwell, the strange thing is that he doesn't seem so geeky any more. He's been back to Beech Bank, and one of the girls whispered to me, "Your stepbrother's quite fit, isn't he!"

I took another look at him. His spots are clearing up, with the help of some medication that Mum discovered. He's had his hair cut in a trendy style and uses gel on it. And he's given up his owl specs and started wearing contact lenses, which bring out the hazel colour of his eyes.

In a couple more years, my stepbrother could be quite a hunk.

# PART FOUR

# Holly's Story

## GO WITH THE FLOW

# one

---

Email from: hollyberry@swiftmail.com
to: scarysarah@hello.com

---

How is the big Oz? Is it as I imagine it 2 B, all sea, surf and sun-bronzed hunx? Have u started school yet? What is your house like? Last question, why did u have to go and emigrate and leave your fave cousin behind all lost and lonely?

Yes, I do miss u loads. I miss coming round with the olds on weekends, and going up to your room 4 all the goss. I miss the sleepovers. I miss sitting up talking 2 U 1/2 the nite, and I miss the yummy cakes your mum used to make. I even miss your smelly feet! (Joke!)

Please email me B 4 I die of loneliness.

Luv,

Your brilliant, beautiful, talented (and modest) fave cousin Holly

P.S. Luv to Auntie, Uncle and David

---

Email from: scarysarah@hello.com
to: hollyberry@swiftmail.com

---

Dear Holly

Sorry it took so long to reply. It's been one mad scrum, getting unpacked, getting settled in. I miss U

2, believe it or not. Haven't been 2 the beach yet, so no chance to check out surfers or other hunx, except some 1 called Wayne who's made friends with David. He's not bad but thinx we are pale Poms and speak funny (He can talk!) Anyway, I want 2 hear about back home, the news on every 1 I know. I think I may B a bit homesick. Write soon.

Luv, Sarah

---

Email from: hollyberry@swiftmail.com
to: scarysarah@hello.com

---

Well, you wanted the news, so here goes. (This may be a v. long email.)

Last Saturday, me, Rach, Wills, Amber and a new girl we've made friends with called Annie (she's cool and you'd like her) went shopping for party stuff. We're having a bash for Chloe at the B.B. Club, it's going to be a HUMUNGOUS surprise! Well, who shld get on the bus but MARK WESTLAKE!!!!! You won't know him, but he's only the FITTEST HUNK EVER! School Football Captain, blond, blue eyes, TOTALLY GORGEOUS! And guess what? He came and sat down beside me, even though he was with some mates.

Needless to say, I thought I'd gone to Heaven! Every 1 in school fancies him. The girls were looking at me like they couldn't believe it, but it was true! Anyway, we got chatting. He knew my name too, so must have noticed me before, even though he's in the 6th Form. The other girls kept peeking and then pretending not to, but I didn't care. I mean, a chance like that may happen only once in a lifetime, don't you agree? Trouble was, my mind seemed to go blank all of a sudden. I tried and tried to think of things to say, kind of cool and witty, but all I could do

was go "Yes," and "No," and "Oh, cool," and feeling like
a complete dork. But it didn't matter, becos he nattered
on about football, and the team, and the position he
plays (wish I'd taken a bit more notice when Dad watches
football on telly) and the different brands of football
boots, etc, etc. He said he was going to watch a big match
in the city, meeting some more mates there. And all the time
the girls were peeking and pretending not to, and Mark's
mates in the back of the bus were chanting "We are the
champions! Yeah yeah yeah YEAH yeah!" and stuff like
that, and my head was spinning.

Anyway, to cut it short (not), before we got to the city,
he asked me what I was doing Saturday evening, casual
like, and I managed to act casual too and said, "Just
hanging out with the girls," and he said, "How about seeing
that film that's on?" I think it's Dark Nights but it could be
Bambi for all I cared, and I said, still casual, "Okay then."
So I have a DATE!!!!! Haven't told Mum and Dad yet, will
face that later.

Got off the bus, walking on air, but Willow brought me
down to earth with a bump. I was watching Mark go off
with his mates, and she tugged my arm and went, "Stop
drooling, Holls, and come on!" So I go, "But I've got a date
with Mark Westlake!"

And she frowned a bit, and then asked me if he was
a Christian. Well, I don't know, but as I told her, I'm not
planning on marrying him (chance would be a fine thing!)

Actually I was quite miffed and let her know it. I mean, I
know she's the big leader and all that but she has no right
to tell me how to run my life. I go to church and I've heard
all that about not being yoked with unbelievers (whatever
that means) but I'm only going out with him for goodness
sake! (I'll write that again – I'm only going out with Mark
Westlake!) Wow!!!! Gasp!!!!

Well, then she said sorry and we made friends, and went to the shops and had a fab time. On the way home, the bus was jam packed and a big fat woman squashed in next to me with a disgusting kid with a runny nose, and Mark was in the back with his mates, all singing looney football songs and hyped-up becos their team had won 6-nil. But, as they say, I had my dreams for company.

Anyway, I said this was going to be a long email, but I am so xited and can't wait until Saturday night! Write and tell me your news. What about this Wayne? Anything to report?

Miss you loads,
Holly

---

Email from: scarysarah@hello.com
to: hollyberry@swiftmail.com

---

Hi Holls

Well, U R the jammy one! I wouldn't have guessed u'd get off with someone like that. Goes 2 show, we never know! As soon as Saturday is over, I want a full report. All details, uncensored! Or else!

I am missing home but beginning 2 settle a bit. Wayne is turning out a bit disappointing. Doesn't surf and has some allergy that means he has to keep out of the sun as much as poss, i.e. cover up when he goes to the beach.

Speaking of beaches, I went to my first beach barbie at the weekend, cool and a bit different to the barbies we used to have in the back garden! Met some cool dudes. Some of them will be at my school.

Must go, hair 2 wash. Don't forget 2 stay in touch. Still missing home. I luv your emails.

Luv, Sarah

# *two*

I missed my cousin Sarah like anything when she and her family emigrated to Australia. Sarah and I are more like sisters than cousins – twin sisters, because there's less than a week's difference in age between us. Sarah's mum and mine actually *are* twins – identical ones, and we've always lived within a mile of each other and spent a lot of time together. Sarah has an older brother David, but I'm a lone kid, and I think I'd have gone nuts after they left if it wasn't for my "girl gang" and the Beech Bank Club.

Out of my group of mates, I'm the only one who's an only child. That has its advantages (more attention, more pocket-money, more everything) but sometimes it can make for problems. For instance, it means that the oldies only have me to focus on. My dad is quite strict (he's a lay-reader and a deacon at church) and my mum is a great worrier. I don't get away with much.

For example, my mum knew something was up the moment I walked through the door the day Mark Westlake asked me out. She was laying the table for dinner when I got in. It's always "dinner" at our house, never "tea" or even "supper". And the three of us sitting round a table, TV off, eating properly with table mats and matching crockery, conversing about the events of the day. Groan! I'd love, just now and then, to crash out with a plate on my lap in front of the telly, like most of my mates do.

Anyway, she was putting out pink table mats and there were pink chrysanths in the middle of the dining table, all tasteful.

"Hello, darling!" she called out as I arrived. "Come and tell me about your day."

So I lugged my shopping bags to the doorway.

"You've had a good day," she said. "You're positively glowing!"

Was it as obvious as all that? I put a hand up to my face and said, "Yeah. Not bad."

"Show me what you bought." So I had to take out the new combats and top and hold them up against myself for her to see. She pulled a little face. "A strange fashion, all those zips and pockets and chains. And the top is a bit skimpy. Nice, though," she added, wanting to be positive.

Mum likes to be encouraging but she wears classical clothes and isn't into teenage fashion. She'd love me to be more like Willow, classy and elegant. Well, too bad. I don't do elegant, even to keep Mum happy.

So I said, "Yes, they're great. And we got loads of party stuff."

She approved of that. Mum helps out at Beech Bank

occasionally, when there's something special on. She's a great cake-baker, (like Sarah's mum), and brilliant at organising and general event-managing.

I'd meant to tell her about Mark, not round the table with Dad there, but when I'd got Mum on her own. Like now. But somehow I didn't. Suddenly I felt shy of talking about the whole thing. I'd been out with boys before, but always as part of a group, going swimming or ten-pin bowling or out for a pizza. Never as a twosome, on our own. And never with someone they didn't know. All of a sudden I wasn't sure what the reaction would be.

So I picked up my bags and headed upstairs. "Don't be long," she called after me. "Dad will be back from golf soon."

Dad is a GP and he plays golf on Saturday afternoons. Sundays are for church and family. I used to go to Sarah's Sunday afternoons but that's changed now. Our lives are very predictable. Boring? Tell me about it!

Not any more. My heart gave a skip and jump as I thought about Mark, his sky-blue eyes, his athlete's physique, the fact that he'd asked me out. I'd have to tell Mum and Dad, of course. But I'd pick the right moment. In the meantime, I'd email Sarah. I felt much better when I'd got it all down online and Sarah had replied. I hadn't mentioned anything at all at dinner. In fact I didn't talk much at all. Dad was going on about his green scores and didn't notice, but Mum kept giving me funny little looks. I began to feel all uncomfortable, almost guilty. Mum has that effect sometimes, even when I haven't done anything. I wanted to get out of there, so after dinner phoned Rachel to see if I could go round to hers. She sounded freaked out and there was a great racket going on in the background. She said all her stepbrothers and sisters were there and she had to stay in. So then I phoned Amber but her dog was sick. Chloe was away and I didn't feel I knew Annie quite well enough to ask to go round to hers just like that.

So that left Willow. I'd left her until last because she'd been a bit iffy about Mark earlier, but by then I was desperate to get out and she sounded as though she'd like to see me. So I went.

I like Willow's house because it's so different to mine. Hers is always a bit of a muddle, both of her parents being slightly hippy-dippy and artistic. I love her room though. Mum got an interior designer in to redecorate mine, but Willow's is all her own work and looks fab. I flopped down with a sigh on her blue bedspread.

"Glad you came," she said. "I felt a bit bad about having a go at you today. Especially since . . ." I knew she was thinking about what had happened at Chadwick's.

"That's history," I said, and meant it. I sighed. "The thing is, Wills, I'm a bit scared of telling Mum and Dad that Mark has asked me out."

Willow was rearranging stuff in her already perfect clothes cupboard. She turned and looked at me. "You'll have to tell them though, Holls."

I sighed again. "Yes, I know. But what if they kick off? You don't know what they're like. What if they try and stop me?"

I was beginning to sound like my own mum, full of worries and what-ifs.

"Pray about it then," said Willow. I might have guessed she'd say that. She gave me another look. "It'll be okay, Holls. As long as you're straight with them. That's the main thing."

I knew she was right. About the praying too. The only thing was, I wasn't sure about this Christian thing any more. I'd gone to church and stuck to the rules all my life. And suddenly I was wondering whether there wasn't more to life. Other people my age had far more freedom to come and go, and weren't hemmed in by rules and regulations. Sometimes it seemed to me they had a far better time of it.

Willow closed the cupboard door. "Shall we get a coffee? Mum and Dad have taken Rowan out to some ceramics exhibition or other. We can chill out by ourselves and listen to some music."

It sounded good. I put my problems to the back of my mind and we went down the cluttered stairs.

# *three*

Sundays are boring since Sarah left. So boring that I'd even taken to going to church twice. Mum and Dad always do, but I sometimes used to skip the evening service and stay on later at Sarah's, unless there was a Youth Service.

That Sunday morning I tried, I really tried, to listen to Rod's sermon, but a face – Mark's – kept coming into my mind, and off I'd go on an imaginary preview of what our date might be like. Would we hold hands going into the cinema? Cuddle up during the film? Would he kiss me, and would I be able to manage it properly? I'd never kissed a boy before, excluding pecks on the cheek from David, which don't count, but I bet Mark had snogged loads of girls. My lips puckered up in anticipation.

"Holly!" There was a hiss in my ear accompanied by a sharp dig in the ribs. Willow was looking at me with disapproval. Everyone was getting up for the last hymn. I scrambled to my feet. Under cover of the first verse, she whispered, "Honestly, what's the matter with you? Pulling strange faces and going all cross-eyed! I bet you never heard a word."

Amber, on the other side, whispered, "I think it's lu-u-urve!" and both of them giggled, though Willow tried not to. That earned us all a dirty look from Mrs Cotterell. Rod and Sadie are cool but some of their congregation are old-fashioned and believe that nothing good can be credited to teenage girls. Mum and Dad were a few seats ahead but Mum has strong radar where I'm concerned and she turned round and gave me one of her looks, which might only seem like a slight raising of the eyebrows to anyone else, but which I know says she expects better of me. That reminded me that I still hadn't said anything to them about my date. Oh dear!

I'd have liked to chill out with Willow and Amber that afternoon, maybe call Rach and Annie and all do something together, but, no, I had to have Sunday lunch as usual with the olds and then go for a nice walk up on the Bluff. I sighed, and longed for Sarah's ear to bend. No point even in emailing her. Nothing new to tell. But at least there was the Youth Service that evening.

The Youth Services are cool. There's a band and a singing group (which I'm in) and we've written some of our own worship songs. Rod usually gives a talk, but it's not like a sermon, more as if he's just chatting to us. And yes, we can butt in if there's something we want to ask or don't understand.

I couldn't believe it when the theme of that evening's talk turned out to be relationships. For a moment I thought Willow must have said something to Rod or Sadie. But a look at her face told me she hadn't. Anyway, Rod talked on about the beauty of the male/female relationship, the blessings of marriage, and how God means that relationship to be a permanent and binding one. I felt myself go all dreamy, wondering what it would be like to be married to Mark.

Rod was saying, ". . . and of course, the Bible makes it very clear that both parties must be equally committed to their relationship with Jesus Christ. Jesus himself taught the importance of that. If not, there won't be true sharing at every level. There can't be, if one has a deep spiritual relationship with Jesus and the other doesn't. Their values and ideas and ambitions will conflict. They'll pull in different directions. And it would mean total confusion for the children."

Now, I'd never got quite as far as imagining myself with children. I suppose I imagined I would one day. I wondered what it would be like to have children with Mark.

Rod was going ". . . of course, not all boy/girl relationships lead to marriage. So as Christians we have to be ultra careful in our choice of friends. It's all too easy to think we can control these friendships, then find we're getting more involved than we intended. So great care is needed." He paused, and seemed to be looking at me. I felt my cheeks grow warm. Could I be quite sure that Willow hadn't been talking? Or one of the others? I pulled myself together. Of course not. Anyway, I was only going on a date. I wasn't committing myself. Nothing wrong with that, was there? Besides, maybe I'd be able to influence Mark, and he'd become a Christian.

"It doesn't work," said Rod, and I almost jumped. "I mean, the idea that we may win others by getting involved with them. What's much more likely is that we'll weaken our own position and get drawn away from our Christian commitment."

I felt a shiver go down my spine. How had he known what I was thinking?

He said a lot more, and then there was a time of discussion, but by then I'd switched off, feeling more and more uncomfortable. I was glad when it was over.

"You don't look very happy, Holls," said Amber as we left the church together.

"Yeah, well, I'm missing my cousin, aren't I," I mumbled, zipping up my jacket.

Willow linked her arm in mine. "Never mind. You've got us. And Rach and Annie and Chloe."

"Not to mention Mark Westlake," said Amber slyly.

Willow was looking thoughtful. "Thinking twice about that, Holls?"

"No. Why should I?" I said huffily, and would have detached myself from Willow if she hadn't been holding on tight.

"No reason," she said. "Except some of the things

Rod was saying. Just go careful, Holls. And don't forget what I said about telling your mum and dad."

Sometimes Willow can be so unbelievably bossy it's unreal. She's worse than a school teacher. "Yes, boss," I said sarcastically. "Any more helpful advice?"

"Not at the moment," she said. And then my mobile rang, and it was Mum worrying again and wondering if Dad should come and pick me up in the car as it was getting dark, and she'd just been watching a TV discussion on knife crime.

"Parents!" I said, and rolled up my eyes, and the other two agreed that they can be one of Life's Greatest Trials, and suddenly we were all friends again.

# *four*

To be honest, I could hardly wait for school to come round. To make it worse, Monday was a day off for teacher training. I spent most of it at the dentist's, having a check-up and dreaming of Mark. I'd read about all the signs of being in love – rapid heartbeat, butterflies in the tummy, loss of concentration – and I was getting the lot. And all because I was going to see Mark again.

I first caught a glimpse of him getting off the bus just as I reached the entrance on Tuesday morning.

He was with some of his mates, messing about and laughing at something. I wondered whether he'd come over and speak to me, and was half excited and half dreading it. Everyone would see.

But he didn't. He just looked kind of sideways at me, sort of half-grinned and then walked off with his friends. A bit of an anti-climax really. The butterflies quietened down and I was left feeling a bit flat. Also ever so slightly annoyed. You don't ask a girl out one day and virtually ignore her three days later. Anyway, during our first period (maths) I got a ticking-off for not concentrating, and at break time Chloe asked me if anything was wrong and I almost snapped at her. If Amber had made any cracks about lu-u-urve I *would* have snapped. But she didn't, fortunately.

At lunchtime, Mark and some of his mates were a few tables away. There were some sixth-form girls at the table too, which gave me a weird feeling. I saw one of them say something into Mark's ear and then playfully ruffle his hair.

"Holly?" said Willow in my ear. "Your eyes are standing out on stalks. Come back to earth."

She was speaking lightly but her green eyes looked full of concern. She knew what was on my mind. Suddenly, I felt my own eyes fill with tears, but I wasn't going to let her see. I got up. "'Scuse me," I said. "I need a bit of air. Back soon."

The other girls had the sense to let me go off on my own. My cheeks were burning as I hurried out of the dining hall and over to the main door. I was furious with Mark, furious with myself for caring so much and making such an idiot of myself. I headed for the clump of beech trees across from the tennis court which gives the school its name. It's out of bounds really, but I didn't care.

It was peaceful among the trees after the racket and clatter of the dining hall. I drew a few deep breaths and began to feel calmer. Then there was the thud of footfalls behind me, and someone called my name. Mark had come after me.

He was standing there grinning with his hair rumpled. I felt my heart flop over.

"Holly?" he said. "You okay, babe? I saw you go storming out. Anything up?"

I shook my head. All confusion was breaking loose inside me. I mumbled, "Just needed some air. Gets hot in there."

He nodded. "Nice to get some space. Come on." He took my hand and led me further into the trees.

I felt as though I was in a dream. The school buildings were left behind and there was just him and me and the fluttering beech leaves in their autumn colours.

"Been thinking about you all over the weekend," he said.

I felt my knees suddenly tremble. I wanted to ask about the blonde girl, but suddenly it didn't seem to matter. He'd left her and he was here with me, wasn't he?

"Still twenty-five minutes of dinner break left," he said. "Let's make the most of it."

And suddenly he pulled me round to the far side of a large beech trunk and was kissing me.

The kiss wasn't at all what I'd expected. I felt awkward and clumsy, although he obviously knew what to do. He'd pushed my head back against the beech trunk and I couldn't draw back. I didn't want things to go this fast. I felt myself freezing up, growing tense. And there was something else. He'd obviously chosen the curry for lunch. Yuck!

I managed to duck away as he came up for air. He seemed put out. "What's the matter? Nobody can see us. Loosen up a bit. Relax and enjoy."

He was coming in for another round. My heart was pounding again. I said, "Don't. Please." I didn't want our first kisses to be like this. And I certainly didn't want his hands beginning to wander all over me, as they were doing now . . .

I pushed his hands away. "Stop it. I don't want this."

He let his hands fall. His blue eyes had a sulky look. "Well. Okay. As you like. I thought you were well up for it though. We'll save it for Saturday, shall we?"

The arrogance of it made me breathless. I'd been all wrong about him. But maybe I'd been giving out the wrong signals too. Either way, I'd been a fool.

I took a deep breath, and said, "Look, I'm sorry. But I'm not sure Saturday's a good idea. Let's forget it."

His face reminded me of a little kid who's had his sweets taken away. Suddenly I felt by far the older of the two of us. He said, "Well, suit yourself. Your loss." And then turned and walked back towards school.

And that was that. I watched him go for a few moments, my thoughts in confusion. I'd made a mistake, big time. What a prize dork I'd been, falling for blue eyes, blonde hair and a sporting reputation. And not much else.

Well, the girls had been right. I was mortified, but not too proud to admit I'd been wrong. Thing was, I couldn't find any of the gang. Then I remembered it was our day for the prayer group.

They were all there when I pushed open the door of the storeroom, even Annie, sitting on their baked bean crates. I tried to look nonchalant. "Hi gang! Sorry I'm late."

But then events caught up all of a sudden, and a big sob came out. They didn't ask any questions, just pulled up another crate for me, sat me down and went on praying. They were praying for one another, for families, for school, for the Beech Bank Club, for our town, even for Amber's dog who was poorly. And for me. That I'd make the right decisions and the right choices. I knew they'd been praying while I was with Mark. And, in spite of my confusion, I knew God had heard, and that he'd already forgiven me for my foolishness. Because he loved me.

# *five*

---

Email from: scarysarah@hello.com
to: hollyberry@swiftmail.com

---

Dear Holls,

How R U? Or, more to the point, where R U? It's 3 days since I've heard and I'm wondrng if U R still on the planet? I started my new school today and it's ok, not quite like school back in the UK. but cool. I have given up on Wayne but met sum 1 called Brad who I like, but Kim (a girl I met at the beach barbie) says watch it, because he has Wandering Hands Syndrome. That's something the boys here suffer from quite a lot apparently. Ha ha!

Anyway, I want to hear from U, so get in touch asap, and that's an order. And don't forget.

With luv and kisses,

Sarah

---

Email from: hollyberry@swiftmail.com
to: scarysarah@hello.com

---

Dear Sarah,

Sorry, sorry, sorry!!! About not emailing. I have no xcuse really except that I've been a bit, well, confused. Or something. To be honest, I've been just like I was when I had chicken-pox (feverish and light-headed) and now I'm like I'm convalescent (loopy but getting back to normal.)

I have to report that there will be no report on Saturday nite, becos there won't be any Saturday nite. Well, there will be Saturday nite, of course, but no date with Mark Westlake. He turned out to be a complete waste of time, one big dsapntmnt, not a partic. nice person. (Ozzie boys are not the only ones with WHS.) And no, I am not saying all this becos he dumped me, becos in fact it was me who dumped him. Saying that makes me feel quite good, so I will repeat it. I DUMPED HIM!!!!!!!!! And no, I don't want to talk about it any more, so don't ask.

Do you know something? As you know, I've always gone to church (or been dragged there more often than not) but although I knew all the right things to say, it didn't always mean much. Sometimes all the rules and do's and don'ts seemed a big drag and I wished I cld be more like other kids whose parents did not force their Christian views upon them. Well, I've changed my views somewhat. Mostly becos of the people at the BB club, and the PG at school. Yesterday when I dumped U no who, they were so cool. They never once said "I told you so," "Serves you right," or any nasty stuff, they were just there for me, kind of supportive and caring. Loving. And suddenly it all got real, God, and the way he loves me with all my faults, and that he's on my side and not just waiting for me to do something wrong so he can punish me for it. I could feel his love like I've never felt it before. So I went and had a long talk with Sadie, and now I feel different about everything. I even feel cool about waiting for God to pick the right boyfriend for me. (Hope he's got some 1 gorgeous lined up!)

Well, I must be getting like my dad becos I've written a long sermon. I wanted to tell you though, becos it means a lot to me and we're still bestest twin cousins, aren't we?

Love,
Holly

---

Email from: scarysarah@hello.com
to: hollyberry@swiftmail.com

---

Dear Holls,

Well, I was a bit gob smacked to get your news, but all I can say is GOOD 4 U!!!!!!! I'm glad you mentioned about the God stuff too. As you know, I didn't have much time for all of that when I was in the UK. And I felt v. sorry for U having to go to church every single Sunday (or even twice!!!)

Well, I've changed my mind, becos some of the guys I met at the barbie, who R in my school 2, have told me that they are Christians. In fact, I went along to a service with them on Sunday night, before going to the beach again. It was cool, great band and everything, not boring at all. And it's strange that you mentioned God being real, becos that's how he seemed to be in that church. And afterwards, when we went to the beach, some of them took their guitars and we just went on singing and having a great time. I got this feeling that God isn't just for church, he's for everyday life, ordinary things, fun times too. Isn't it just something?

Anyway, I'm going to hang in there and find out more. I'm not quite so homesick now, though I still miss you loads of course. But it'll be interesting to see what happens for both of us. And we'll have the best time ever when U come over next year! Can't wait!!!

Hugs and kisses
From your "twin"
Sarah

# PART FIVE

# Amber's Story

## DRAMA QUEEN

# *one*

Holly is always on about her cousin Sarah, and how much she misses her since she went to Australia, and how they're actually almost twins. I used to be a bit envious about being that close to a family member. I have two sisters but Kim is twenty-one and at uni and the other, Lucy, is only five years old. She is quite cute and we all love her to bits, although I think she's very spoilt and gets away with murder. My dad says I'm only jealous because I don't like someone else getting the attention. As if! I could actually do with a bit less sometimes of the kind of attention I get from them! Like cross-examining me whenever I'm three-and-a-half minutes late, or wanting to know every detail of my day (especially when I'm hanging out with mates) or not letting me put a lock on my bedroom door, which they say is unsafe in case of fire, but which I know is just so they can barge in whenever they feel like it, without any regard for my need for privacy! They tell everyone Lucy is their "afterthought" which is *so* sick-making and makes my toes curl with embarrassment! In fact, my parents are embarrassing all round. My mum will insist on doing an aerobics

DVD, and carries on practising even in front of my friends, and I sometimes think my dad has scary Homer Simpson tendencies! But to be fair, they've got good points. They don't earn a lot of money (Mum's a dinner lady and Dad's a fork-lift driver) but they try to give us kids the best they can, like going to uni.

Anyway, where was I? Oh yes, talking about twins. I don't have a twin sister or cousin, but what I do have is a twin dog. Or had. Because he's no longer with us and I'm devastated.

Barney was actually born the same day as me, though he didn't join our family until three months later. Kim was seven then, my brothers Charlie and Sam were nine and five, and all of them had apparently been pleading for a dog for ages. Mum says Sam burst into tears when he saw me for the first time – he'd hoped for a puppy! Anyway, my parents took pity on them and added Barney to the family menagerie.

I don't ever remember Barney not being there. He and I grew up together. He was a mixture kind of dog, with longish brown hair, deep brown eyes and a long wavy tail that I was always trying to grab hold of. My mother says I would lean from my high chair and feed Barney with my mashed vegetables, a spoonful for him and one for me, alternately. He was always trying to lick my messy hands and face clean at mealtimes. And when I began to crawl I once crept into his basket and they found us curled up asleep together. It all sounds most unhygienic to me, and when I mentioned this, my brother Sam said that it was okay, Barney had a healthy constitution and managed to avoid catching anything nasty from me. Very funny! (not!)

Barney trotted beside the pushchair when we went for walks, and later he was always there at the school gates with Mum waiting when I came out of school. He always came on outings with us too, although we had to be careful because he was sometimes travel sick. All of us tried to avoid sitting next to him in the car, although at home watching TV we liked to sit beside him, he was so warm and comfortable to lean on, and smelt lovely when he'd been recently bathed. (Not so nice when he'd been rolling on a dead fish he found down by the river!) Barney was patient with us kids and never once snapped or growled at us, although there was one particular postman he took a dislike to and who finally refused to come to our house any more. Charlie said the postman must be a suspect person, that dogs can sense these things.

Anyway, Barney was part of our family, part of the furniture, part of the very fabric of our lives. (I read that in a library book and thought it was a nice phrase!) He'd had a few illnesses and was once run over by a delivery van but always got over everything. Therefore I wasn't too concerned when I got in from shopping with the girls the Saturday we bought Chloe's birthday balloons and was met by Lucy, looking important.

"Barney's poorly," she told me. "He had to go to the doctor's."

"I think you mean the vet," I said. I was dying to try on the new T-shirt I'd bought, but I went through to the kitchen to see Barney. He was in his basket, lying nose on paws with his eyes shut. He did open his eyes to look at me and thumped his tail when I bent down to pat him. His nose felt warm and I noticed for the first time how grey around the muzzle he'd got.

"Is he really ill?" I asked Mum, who was peeling potatoes at the sink. I thought she'd say it was nothing much, but instead she hesitated and then said, "Well, he might be. He's started on an antibiotic, and it may be just a touch of pneumonia, but the vet did some other tests too."

She didn't say what the tests were for, but it sounded bad. I felt the first twinge of alarm. "But he won't die, will he?" Again she hesitated, with a glance at Lucy. My alarm intensified. "Mum?"

She said, "We must remember he's an old dog. He's fourteen, Amber. That's old for a dog. He can't go on for ever."

Now I thought about it, Barney had been much slower just lately. He slept a lot and seemed stiff sometimes. It was a long time since he'd chased a stick or had a run-in with the next-door cat.

But Barney dying – it was unthinkable. It couldn't happen. I wouldn't let it. I'd take care of Barney and get him through this. I wouldn't give up on him, even if everyone else did. I patted him and said, "Good old Barney! I'm here now, and you'll be okay."

He looked at me sadly and heaved a sigh. I felt my eyes fill with tears.

That evening I gave Barney all his favourite tit-bits. He wasn't really interested but ate one or two to please me. Later, Holly phoned wanting me to go over to hers, but I explained and said I had a sick dog who needed my attention. I thought of sitting up all night with him, but Mum got cross and shooed me off to bed. Everyone was going on just as usual, telly on, Lucy shrieking, Mum and Dad arguing about what colour they should pick to paint the bathroom. No one seemed to care a bit.

Next day, Barney seemed a little bit better. The antibiotics were obviously working. I heaved a big sigh of relief and went off to meet the girls for church. Crisis over, I thought.

Wrong. By next morning, Barney was weak and listless again, lying curled in his basket.

It was both Mum and Dad's day off, and they were planning some decorating. "We'll call at the vet's first though," said Mum, putting a band on Lucy's hair. "Test results might be in."

"I'll stay home with him," I said.

"You will not," said Mum. "And you're late, so hurry up."

There was nothing else for it. At school, Holly was acting moonstruck over Mark, and everyone was giving their opinions. It was Rachel who noticed I was quiet and asked me what was wrong, and then said, "Well, it's our prayer day. So let's pray about Barney."

I hadn't thought about that. Did God care about dogs? Could he make sick ones well? I didn't really know, but the thought made me feel a whole lot better, so much better that, after the prayer group, I stopped worrying altogether. I almost expected to see Barney come galloping down the path to meet me when I got home. Instead, there was Mrs Watson next door, hovering near the garden fence and waiting for me. Our house seemed to be deserted.

"There you are, dear," said Mrs Watson. "Your mum asked me to look out for you."

"Where are they all?" I asked. "They're meant to be painting the bathroom."

Mrs Watson looked away from me, and began to nip some dead heads off her roses.

"They're – er – they're at the vet's," she said.

"But they can't have been there all day," I said.

"Well dear, I expect they'll explain everything when they get home," said Mrs Watson, and I could tell that something was up.

And then I knew. A cold feeling started in my chest and spread through my body, and I rushed into our house and slammed the door.

The test results had shown that Barney had a terminal illness. He would get worse and he'd suffer. Badly. Much better to let him go quietly to sleep, the vet had said.

"He never suffered," said Mum later. "Just drifted away very easily, while Dad and I stroked his head and told him what a good dog he was."

We buried Barney in the garden, under the apple tree where he used to lie on hot days. I cried and cried, angry, grief-stricken, guilty. "I never even said goodbye! You could have waited and let me come too!"

Mum reached out and stroked my cheek. "We thought it better this way, quickly and quietly, without any fuss. He had a good life, Amber. A happy one. Let's remember that and be glad. And one day maybe we'll get another dog."

I pulled away, resentful and bitter. "I don't want another one! I loved Barney! I can't forget him, just like that, even if the rest of you can! I don't want another dog! Never! Not ever!"

## *two*

Did I mention that my brother Charlie is training to be a vet? He is in his fourth year of vet training – or is it his fifth? I get muddled up because it takes so long, seven years in all before you are a fully qualified veterinary surgeon, two years longer than it takes to qualify as a doctor. So that means animals are more complicated and therefore more important people than humans, doesn't it? I think so anyway, at least most of the time. I would quite like to be a vet too, but I'm not sure I could stick *seven* years (half my present lifetime!) learning about the innards of cows and horses and all the nasty parasites and things that animals pick up.

It was Charlie who first mentioned that dogs quite often look like their owners, or vice versa (this was before Barney died) and this set me off thinking of my friends and what kind of dog they should have. Some of them have dogs already, for instance, Rachel's family have a great big Labrador. Rachel really ought to have a little Yorkshire terrier because that's the way she is, small and bright-eyed and bouncy, with short legs (though I'd never say that to her face). Holly's dog would have to be a Bichon Frise, a pretty little dog, and Willow's would be an Irish setter, red-haired and long-legged and elegant. Barney suited me fine because he had long brown hair and brown eyes and a lovely disposition (ha ha!) and I thought Annie was quite like an intelligent border collie now that she'd stopped running like a nervous greyhound. Chloe was the one I puzzled over most. She is slim and blonde, and would be quite stunning if she'd just hold herself upright and be confident and realise just what a special person she is.

It was Chloe who phoned me first when Barney died. I didn't tell anyone what had happened the day after, although all of them wanted to know why I went to school all red in the face and with my eyelids swollen from crying all night. I didn't want to go at all, but Mum said I had to face people, that life goes on and that I would learn to live with it and a lot of other bracing things. I thought she and Dad were well hard-hearted about the whole thing, and even Lucy seemed to forget about poor old Barney when Mum got out a new Dora the Explorer bag for school. I felt I would never, ever, forgive them for murdering Barney with never a word to me.

Anyway, I told the other girls I had a cold coming on and that's why I was sniffing a lot. They all swallowed it except Chloe, who gave me a funny look. And then she phoned me after school, when I was in my room having yet another weep into my soggy pillow.

"It's Barney, isn't it, Ams," she said while I was wiping my streaming eyes. "He's worse."

"He's dead," I said, and burst into tears again. "Yesterday, when I was at school, they – they had him killed!"

I sobbed and sobbed, while she made soothing noises into the other end of the phone. Then she said, "Shall I come over?" and I said, "No, it's all right. There's nothing you can do, and anyway, we've got a pile of maths homework. But thanks for offering."

Then I sobbed some more, until I heard Chloe's dad asking if she was talking on the landline and if so, would she kindly remember who paid the bill, and she said no, she was on her mobile, and I thought again how horrid and heartless parents can be, regarding everything in terms of money and not realising how deeply we feel our losses. And that set me off again, and there didn't seem much point on carrying on a conversation that was all sobbing on one end and "there there" kind of remarks on the other, so we said goodbye and that we'd text each other in a little while. But I was grateful to Chloe for caring.

Anyway, the reason I mentioned Charlie was that the following weekend Mum told me he was coming home from vet school for a quick visit. I'm always pleased to see Charlie, but I knew from the way she said it that she thought I'd get over my grief immediately and be on top of the world again. As if! It's asking a bit much when your *twin* has died. But they don't understand at all. The night before, I'd gone across to the bathroom for a drink of water and heard them talking about me in their bedroom. Of course, I stopped to listen when I heard my name mentioned.

Mum asked, "How long is she going to keep this up, do you think?" and Dad said, "Well, you know what a drama queen she is. We all feel bad about it, but you'd think it was one of her brothers the way she's carrying on."

Mum said, "Maybe we should have waited until she could come with us to the vet's – maybe she would have felt better," and Dad said, "Not on your life! Can you imagine the scene? Bad enough having to do it – and pay through the nose – without a hysterical fourteen year old throwing a wobbly." And then they *laughed!* Actually *laughed,* when there'd been a *death* in the family! And that crack about brothers, when Barney was actually my *twin*!

Well, next morning I gave them the silent treatment to show my utter contempt for their heartless attitude. They didn't seem to notice. Dad was late for work and Mum was in a tizz over Charlie coming, thinking about beds and making a list of the extra shopping we'd need. Barney's basket had been removed. It was as though he'd never existed. It made me feel sick.

At school, word had got round and I must say the girls were quite sympathetic. Afterwards we went to Beech Bank and Sadie had a little word too and told me how sorry she was. And while she was speaking, I noticed Chloe's eyes filling with tears, as though she really cared. Later, I decided that I realised what kind of dog Chloe was. A cocker spaniel, with big sad eyes, who was happy when everyone it loved was happy, and miserable when they were not.

# three

Charlie came home on Friday evening. After he'd called the evening before, Mum said mysteriously that he'd be bringing someone else with him. She wouldn't say who, just to be irritating. I had a bit of a grouse because I thought I'd have to squeeze in with Lucy to make room, but she said I didn't have to. So my imagination quickly got to work, wondering who it might be. One of his mates from vet school? If that was the case, I'd have all the girls casually dropping by to check him out. They'd probably do that anyway, because all of them considered Charlie to be well fit and a mature man as well, being twenty-three. Or it might be a new girlfriend. I wasn't sure how I'd feel about that. He'd brought girls home before, some a bit iffy and some who were babes, and others who fell somewhere in between. None of them lasted long. It would be interesting to see what this latest one was like.

Well, it wasn't a girlfriend. It wasn't a mate. It turned out to be a puppy, a tiny, scraggy little black-and-white thing with fluffy bits on its ears. I took one look at him and felt like bursting into tears again. This was all Mum's doing. She thought I'd forget Barney, just like that, if another dog came along.

Lucy was thrilled to bits, looking ready to kill the dog with kindness or squeeze it to death, or both. Mum and Dad seemed a little more restrained, looking at me out of the corners of their eyes to see how I was reacting. Dad picked him out of the travelling basket and held the pup up to look at him. The pup was trembling a bit. Mum looked at me and said encouragingly, "He seems a nice little chap, doesn't he, Amber?"

They weren't going to get round me like that! I said huffily, "Don't ask me. Charlie's the expert. It's his dog."

I knew very well it wasn't, that this creature was meant to replace Barney. Mum and Dad and Charlie looked at each other. Charlie was looking rather cool, with his fair hair gelled up and a new Ralph Lauren shirt.

"It isn't mine," he said. "This little mutt was left at the vet's surgery where I've been helping out weekends. He's the last of an abandoned litter. When Mum told me about poor old Barney, I thought – well, I thought it wouldn't hurt for you all to take a look at him."

I knew what he'd thought. What they'd all thought. Get Amber a new dog and she'll quit moping and forget about the old one. As if!

I said huffily, "Well, it's nothing to do with me. My opinion's never asked anyway. Just do as you think best, same as usual."

And I swept upstairs, with my head in the air, and stayed there until dinner time. Let them call me a drama queen if they liked. At least I wasn't a heartless traitor!

By the time Charlie left on Sunday evening, the puppy had begun to make itself at home. They at least had the grace not to give it Barney's old basket, but got a new, smaller one. The puppy was lonely at first; several times I heard it yipping in the night when it was left on its own. Charlie got up to it at first, then Mum or Dad. It didn't like new places or new people, and trembled when there was a sudden noise like a door banging. Lucy loved it and would sit by the basket for hours stroking it and crooning to it. I was reminded of myself and Barney, and felt bereaved all over again. I had as little as possible to do with the pup, though Mum and Dad tried hard to get me involved.

"Can you think of a name for him?" Dad asked, when Charlie had left. "We can't go on calling him Pup for ever."

"Inky Pinky Fluffy Wuffy?" suggested Lucy.

"That's a bit of a mouthful," said Dad. "We need a nice short name. Like Bob. Or Patch. Or – what do you think, Amber?"

I shrugged indifferently. "It doesn't matter to me what it's called," I said coldly. The pup looked up at me and wagged its ridiculous stumpy tail hopefully, its head on one side. I ignored it and gathered my clean school uniform together to take upstairs, leaving Lucy to half-strangle the pup.

Nothing's a secret for long in our school. By next day, everyone knew we'd got a new puppy at our house. The girls wanted to come round and see it, and in fact Holly and Chloe did come. They sat on the floor, cooing over it and talking silly baby talk to it until I felt ready to vomit.

"Such a little sweetie, isn't ums?" said Holly. The pup licked her face and she squealed. So then Chloe tickled him and he licked her face too.

"I'd be careful if I were you," I said frostily. "It's too young to have had all its inoculations yet. You could catch worms or some dreadful disease."

"Is Amber a grumpy-wumpy old thing then?" said Holly. Chloe looked at me and said, "Don't you like him then, Ams?"

"I have no feelings about it whatsoever," I said. "And if we're going to Beech Bank, we'd better be off."

# *four*

That weekend we had Film Night at the Beech Bank Club. They have them every so often, on a huge screen at the end of the big room. Some of the films are cool, but sometimes they rake up some that are dated and old-fashioned, the kind of thing my parents would go for. This one was a real oldie, called *The Hiding Place*, and was about a Dutch lady called Corrie ten Boom, who hid Jews in a tiny little cupboard in her bedroom during World War Two, and was put into a concentration camp by the Nazis. I didn't think I'd like it at all, but found it really grabbed me after a bit, though it was very harrowing in parts. Rachel and

Chloe were in floods most of the time, when Corrie's sister was dying, for instance.

All of us talked about it on the way home, and we kept on talking when the others had branched off and it was just Holly and Chloe and me. Chloe was still inclined to sniff a bit, like when we remembered Corrie and her sister's last words to each other.

Holly was impressed with the way God had concealed the two women when a search was going on.

"What did you think, Ams?" asked Chloe.

I thought for a bit and then answered as honestly as I could. The part that had struck me most was right at the end, when the war was long over and the survivors released, and Corrie met one of the guards who had been a real brute to her and her sister. He said he had become a Christian and asked her forgiveness for what he'd done and held out his hand to her. Corrie could not take it, but suddenly a sense of God's mercy swept over her and she found herself clasping the man's hand and saying she forgave him.

"I don't know how she could," I said, remembering the horrors they'd been through. "I'm sure I couldn't."

"I guess it was God's doing," said Holly. "He really helped her do what he tells us we have to do – love our enemies and forgive those who hurt us and all that."

I felt a bit strange all of a sudden. Corrie ten Boom had forgiven somebody who'd been a real beast, and there was me holding a big grudge and refusing to forgive my parents, who I felt had hurt me badly but who on the whole had been reasonable parents most of my life, though sometimes a bit off this planet. They meant well. That's what they said, and I had no reason to disbelieve it.

So I stopped in the middle of the road, and said, "I think I've just had a revelation!"

Both of them looked at me and Holly rolled up her eyes. "What are you on about now?"

"I think God has spoken to me," I said.

"What did he say?" they both asked together.

"Well, I didn't hear actual words," I admitted. "But that isn't always how it happens, is it? But I've just suddenly realised – Corrie was able to forgive that man because she knew Jesus forgave all her sins when he died on the Cross. And," I paused. This was getting personal, but I might as well get it off my chest. The girls were looking at me all agog, wondering what was coming next.

I went on, "For just the same reason, we have to forgive people who've done wrong to us." I paused again. They looked at me expectantly, knowing there was more to come.

"And?" prompted Chloe.

"And," I said, "I've just realised I am doing that very thing! Refusing to forgive Mum and Dad over Barney. And – " another pause "even worse, I've been taking it out on that poor little Hamlet, who never did any harm to anybody."

For a moment the two of them looked at me as though I'd really flipped my lid.

"Er – who is Hamlet?" asked Holly after a moment.

"The new puppy," I said. "Just an innocent, harmless little creature in need of love, who I should have been taking to my heart instead of ostrichising it."

"Don't you mean ostracising?" asked Chloe.

"Whatever," I said. "Anyway, I can see it all now. The scales have fallen from my eyes. I've seen the light!"

"Does that mean you'll be saying sorry to your mum and dad then?" asked Holly, as we began to walk on.

"Er – well, yes, I expect so," I said. That was going to be the hard bit. I still felt sore inside over Barney, and I still felt they could have acted differently. But, hey, God had helped Corrie forgive a brutal inhuman Nazi, and he would surely help me with this. I squared my shoulders and said, "Yes, I will be apologising. Profusely. Should I go down on my knees, do you think?"

"Maybe not," said Holly. "They're getting on in years, you don't want to give them a turn. No need to go OTT. Let us know how you get on."

I promised I would. And I was determined to be nice to Hamlet, too, to make up for the horrible attitude I'd shown him before. He wouldn't be my twin as Barney was, but I could be a kind of foster-mother to him, someone he would adore and look up to.

We had arrived at my gate. The lights were on in the sitting room. I knew that Lucy would be in bed. Now would be the time to make my dramatic apology.

"Just tell me one thing," I said, with my hand on the gate latch. Chloe and Holly looked at each other, wondering what was coming now.

"Do you think I'm a drama queen?" I asked.

Both of them grinned and rolled up their eyes again.

"Just a bit," said Holly. "But we love you just the same."

# *five*

Well, I did the apologising bit, eating humble pie and all that. Maybe I overdid it just a bit. Mum and Dad seemed a little mystified. At one stage Mum said, "Of course we forgive you, love. We've said so at least three times," and Dad said, "No need to make a meal of it. We get the message," which I thought was rather tactless, but then Dad is not the most sensitive of persons as I may have mentioned before.

I ended up my remarks by saying, "And I've decided to fully accept Hamlet into the family."

Mum and Dad looked blank, and Mum said exactly what Holly had. "Er – who is Hamlet?"

I flung my hand out to the pup, fast asleep in his basket. "Him. Well, you did ask me to name him."

"Well, yes. But we thought you weren't interested," said Dad. "We'd just about made up our minds that Ruff might be a nice name, because of the ruffly bits around his neck and ears . . ." Then he caught Mum's eye, and said quickly, "But Hamlet is fine. Hamlet will do very nicely. Yes."

I was almost sure I heard them laughing as I closed the door, but I didn't mind. I went to bed and to sleep right away, with none of the sad dreams I'd been having about Barney coming galloping across a meadow to meet me, and then waking up and sobbing into my pillow.

I slept late, and when I woke the sun was shining and a great load seemed to have lifted from my heart. I'd often wondered what that meant but now I knew. It did really feel as though the heavy lump of sadness I'd carried inside had melted and gone.

I got dressed and went downstairs to a deserted house and a note on the fridge. Dad had taken the car into the garage for a service, dropping off Mum and Lucy at ballet class. Only the puppy, Hamlet, was there, asleep in his basket. He woke and looked warily at me while I was eating my cornflakes. Now was the time to do some bonding. He'd already been fed, but I gave him some milk and he lapped it up. Then we went out into the garden.

Hamlet was really a pretty little thing when you

looked at him properly. He had black markings on the white coat, and the fluffy bits on his ears gave him a pixie look. I found an old rubber ball and threw it for him to fetch. He sat down and looked at the ball and then at me. Well, maybe he didn't understand balls yet. I sat down beside him and patted him, but he inched nervously away from me. His tail didn't wag and his brown eyes looked worried.

"Look," I said, "I'm very sorry I was horrid to you before, but we're friends now. You're going to be our dog. There's nothing to be scared of. We're your family."

He didn't believe me. He trembled a bit and edged further away. I sighed. This bonding session wasn't going too well. I couldn't help being a bit disappointed. Maybe this dog had some deep psychological problem – did dogs get those? I'd have to ask Charlie about it.

I decided we'd give each other some space for a bit and got to my feet. White chrysanthemums and purple asters were blooming in the flower beds. I picked a bunch of them and carried them down to the apple tree where Barney's grave was. I saw that someone – it must have been Dad – had put up a small, simple wooden cross with Barney's name and dates on it in neat black lettering. The sight of it made a big lump come up in my throat. It wasn't just me who had loved Barney and who missed him now.

Hamlet hadn't followed me. Walking back up the garden, I saw him sitting there on the patio where I'd left him, a lonely, pathetic, vulnerable little patch of white.

And then I saw something else too. The ginger cat from next door had come over and was hiding in the long grass near the fence, keeping its eye on Hamlet and creeping nearer.

Barney and the cat had been bitter enemies. I remembered numerous fights between then, spitting and snarling and yapping affairs, with Barney chasing the cat all round the garden. These spats usually ended with the cat up a tree or on the fence, swearing horribly with ears laid back at a frantically yapping dog below. Neither of them quite lost these battles and neither quite won. It was frustrating for them both, and the more they battled the more they hated each other.

And now Barney was gone and the cat had targeted Hamlet, poor little scaredy orphaned Hamlet, who hadn't a chance of defending himself. As I watched, the cat pounced, raking out sharp claws at the pup. It was as though at last he felt he could get his own back for all the frustrating outcomes of the scraps that had taken place in our garden.

Ginger's Revenge, I thought, and began to run. Hamlet gave a terrified squeak and half-scrambled, half-rolled down the patio steps. The cat was twice his size and must have been a fearsome sight. I yelled and flapped my arms. For a moment there seemed to be just a moving ball of ginger and white, with bits of fur beginning to fly. Then the cat detached itself and sprang for the wall. Hamlet crouched terrified in the grass. A streak of blood showed on his nose. Then he saw me and came scrambling towards me, whimpering and burrowing into my arms as I flung myself down. I held his trembling little body and murmured soothingly.

After a bit the trembling lessened. The cat had scratched his nose but I didn't think he was harmed otherwise. I stood him up and his legs were okay. He looked up at me and then his little pink tongue came out and licked my hand. When I got up, he trotted after me trustingly.

We spent the morning together, chilling out in the sun and exploring the scents of the garden. Once he trusted you, the pup changed character completely. He wanted all the attention he could get, and would do anything to get it, rolling over and over, chasing everything that moved, chewing on anything – including fingers and toes – yipping squeakily at beetles and creepy crawlies, grabbing the hems of my jeans and worrying away at them. Anything to get attention. Quite a little drama queen, in fact.

# PART SIX

# Chloe's Story

## THE MIRACLE

# one

My birthday was coming up, and once again, I wished I was like all the others and could have a real party. There was nothing I wanted more – well, except for one thing. Mostly the others had sleepovers on their birthdays. On Holly's fourteenth, we'd all dressed up and her dad and mum had taken us out to dinner and to see *Joseph* at the theatre. It was magic. Then we'd gone back to hers to spend the night, all of us sleeping in her big posh room at her big posh house. Two of us had squashed into Holly's bed, two more on the sofa bed, and two on blow-up airbeds. There was bags of room for everyone. We were tired and went to sleep quite soon, and in the morning Holly's mum had breakfast all set out for us; grapefruit, cereal, bacon and eggs, toast and marmalade, the works. And then we all went to church together.

Rachel had a sleepover too, and it was quite different because all her steps were there as well, and we had sleeping bags crammed all over the house so that whenever we got up we stepped on some body or other, and none of us could stop giggling, and there were crisps and crumbs and sweet wrappers everywhere next day. At Amber's sleepover we were up half the night telling each other spooky stories, and then her big sister took us all out for brunch and a makeover. Annie and Willow hadn't had their birthdays yet, but I knew they'd be doing special things too, and we'd all get to share the fun.

I was always the odd one out. I suppose I must have had birthday parties once, when I was little and before Mum died. Things were normal then. They hadn't been normal for a long time now. I'd never had a sleepover, never even had a party at home, or had the girls over, except Amber once or twice. They'd asked to come, but I made excuses and in the end I think they got the message and stopped asking. They stayed friends with me though, and I was glad of that.

Amber was the one who came nearest to guessing the truth.

"It's about your brother, isn't it?" she said one evening, when she'd asked to come round to do homework together, and I'd quickly arranged to go to hers instead.

I felt myself tense up, and said quickly, "What do you mean?"

"It's about Peter," she said. "Why you can't ask people round." She paused and said, "Look, Clo, I'm not being nosey, but, well – we're here for you, all of us. Or just me, if you'd rather. It might help to talk. If there's a problem."

I didn't answer for a moment. This was my cue to

come clean, to share the heavy load that often seemed too much for me to carry. I'd often longed to talk to the girls but I was scared to – scared that they wouldn't understand, that they'd be shocked, that they'd reject me if they knew the truth. And I needed them more than anything else in the world.

I felt my eyes fill with tears. Amber swivelled her seat round from the computer screen and jumped up to come and hug me. "Clo, it's all right. Maybe we can help."

I shook my head. "No, nobody can."

"Oh, Clo!" She seemed near to tears herself. "I do understand. I think I can guess what's wrong. Peter's ill, isn't he?"

I nodded and gulped. "Sort of." I realised there was no point in denying it. Everybody must know that Peter was often ill and off school, sometimes in hospital.

"I do understand," she said again. "I know what it is to suffer when someone's ill, Clo. I did when Barney got sick and died. And you really helped me then. Now I want to help you."

That almost made me smile. Amber's such a drama queen, but I know she really loved her dog. But I said again, "You can't help me, Ams. Nobody can."

She wouldn't give up though. She looked at me for a moment, then she said, "Look, Clo. I think I know what's going on. I've read a lot of medical books – well, they're vet ones really, but a lot of animal diseases are the same as human ones. I think I know what's wrong with Peter. It's to do with the immune system, isn't it. It's – it's leukaemia."

I stared at her, absolutely dumbstruck, not knowing whether to laugh or cry. We'd kept very quiet about Peter's condition, Dad and Peter and I, hadn't breathed a word outside the family. It was bad enough knowing what we knew, without everyone else knowing it too. Mainly because Peter himself was so devastated by it.

"It's not fair, Clo," he'd said to me over and over. "It's just not fair." And I agreed.

And now Amber had read some vets' textbook and come to her own conclusions. "I'm right, aren't I, Clo?" she asked quietly.

And suddenly I felt the tears spilling over and running down my cheeks, and I was nodding, and Amber was hugging me tight and saying, "It'll be okay, Clo. It'll be okay. We'll pray. We'll all pray."

I stiffened up then and pulled away. "No! You're not to tell anyone, Ams! Not even the other girls. I promised Peter. He – he gets really depressed and he'd hate it if people knew – you've got to promise."

She looked a bit surprised but she did promise. And to be fair, I don't think she did say a word to the others.

Walking home, I felt rather strange. In a way, it was a huge relief that Amber was sharing this with me. I'd felt very alone for a long time. But there was also a nagging guilt and something else I couldn't quite describe. I was glad of Amber's sympathy and caring, but I wasn't sure I'd still have it if she knew the whole truth. Her conclusions had been near the mark, but not quite right. I'd lied to her, in effect. It wasn't leukaemia Peter had, it was HIV.

# two

I've always wanted to be a writer, right from when I was a little girl and discovered that words could make me laugh, or cry, or take me to other places and other times. I started early on, writing my own stories. I kept diaries and journals and made notes for when I would write really big stuff, like best-selling novels. I was sure I'd be a real writer one day.

Peter had always wanted to be a footballer, but he'd given that up two years ago. It wasn't likely to happen now. That hurt him more than anything.

It wasn't even his fault, that was the worst thing of all. Almost three years ago, when Peter wasn't much older than I am now, and the star of the local under-sixteens team, he'd gone to play in an away match against another club. They'd won and were coming home in the mini-bus, shouting and singing and having a rare old time. It was dark and getting late, and suddenly another mini-bus full of another lot of football supporters came from the opposite direction. Only these were men, and they'd been drinking; even the driver, who rounded a bend far too fast, lost control and skidded head-on into Peter's bus. It was horrendous, the drunk driver died and a lot of the passengers from both buses were seriously injured. There was blood everywhere. Peter had cuts on his hands and face and he was dazed, but he was one of the lucky ones. He and a couple of others were the ones who called for help and then tried their best to help the others until the ambulances and police came. Afterwards, he was one of three boys commended for their presence of mind. They had saved at least one life.

But it was at a huge price. After the accident, they said Peter had something called Post Traumatic Stress Syndrome, which gave him terrible headaches and made him depressed. And later still, they found that he tested HIV positive from contact with infected blood.

I wasn't quite eleven at the time. Mum had died before I was four and I didn't remember her really. It had been Dad and Peter and me for ages. I'd stayed with Auntie Sue for a while, but was so badly homesick that Dad brought me home again.

I thought things would get back to normal again but they never did. Peter was moody and quiet, but sometimes got into furious rages, when he'd smash things and throw things about. Dad explained to me about HIV and what it meant. He said that there had been great progress with treatment and that Peter could have a good future, but I cried and cried and thought my heart would break.

I don't know what would have happened if I hadn't changed schools just then and started going to Beechwood High. On the very first day I met Amber, and we found we lived quite near together. In a few weeks, we'd made friends with Rachel and then Willow and Holly. For a while there was Kate too, but she moved away after the first year. So we were five, but then Annie came and we were six again. With the girls, I could sometimes forget what had happened.

Not at home though. A few of Peter's friends stuck by him but most gradually dropped off one by one.

"I'm a freak," he said to me one day. He had the haunted look in his eyes that meant he was beginning to dip down into depression. He'd been a cool-looking guy but didn't care much about his appearance any more.

"What's the point," he would say. "Nobody'd want to know me if they knew. What's the point of living at all?"

It frightened me, that kind of talk. I tried hard to be positive, told him over and over again that he'd get over the PTSS, all the doctors said so, it only needed time.

"Which I may not have," he said bitterly, and sighed, and I felt my own heart sink.

"That medication will keep you well," I said desperately. "And there's research going on all the time. They might find a permanent cure some time soon."

Both of us had searched the Internet and we knew the score.

"You can't just give up," I said. "You can't. Peter . . ." I could feel my throat closing up.

Peter looked at me sadly. "Sorry, Clo. I don't mean to upset you." He got up and walked heavily upstairs. I heard some sad music start to play.

I cried and cried.

It was around then that I began to go to the Beech Bank Club with the others. For the very first time, I heard things that gave me a flicker of hope. These people believed in God. They said that God cared about all of us. That we could pray to him about anything.

"Are you sure?" I asked Sadie that very first night. "I mean, *everything*? I mean, okay, so God made the world and all that, but surely he can't listen to every single person that decides to pray."

With Peter so often depressed, Dad and I had agreed that it was better not to talk about the exact nature of his illness. Peter hated the thought of people knowing anyway. So I'd told the girls nothing.

"Everything," said Sadie, and gave me a keen look. "Was there something in particular, Chloe?"

"No," I said quickly. "I was just curious."

But I did begin to pray, alone and secretly and desperately, with many tears, pleading with God to help Peter, to make him well, to make him happy again, to let the HIV be some mistake, to lift the depression, to perform a miracle.

## *three*

They had a library at the Beech Bank Club. You could borrow a book and take as long as you liked to read it, or you could buy it for a small sum if you wanted to keep it. I thought at first they might be boring "religious" books, but soon found how wrong I could be. Before long I was borrowing three or four a week, buying some so that I could read them again and again. I gobbled and devoured them, some fiction and stuff for teenage girls, but also biographies like *Chasing the Dragon* and *Run, Baby, Run*. Those real-life stories made me realise that God is alive and involved with people in a way I'd never imagined. I don't know quite how or when it happened, but before long I knew I'd stopped doubting and begun to believe.

Peter was angry though. "Don't give me that God stuff!" he said bitterly when I tried to explain. "There isn't any God, and if there is, he's cruel and he's unfair. What about all the suffering in the world? What about floods and famines, and wars and suicide bombings? What about all the sick people? Why do those things happen if God's in charge of the world?"

I knew he was thinking of his own situation too. I had no answers for him. I couldn't understand why any of those things happen either. All I knew was that when I thought about God, or read about him, or prayed to him, I was getting this amazing peaceful feeling, as though, against all the odds, everything would be all right.

My birthday was coming up and I'd been dreading it. A few weeks before, Dad asked, rather hesitantly, "What do you fancy doing on your birthday this year, Chloe?"

I felt sorry for him. Like lots of men, he's really hopeless when it comes to understanding daughters, or teenage girls, or any kind of female really. I had to go to Auntie Sue when I needed my first bra, or advice about periods, or buying clothes, or most other things for that matter. I get the feeling he half thinks I'm still a little girl in the Barbie and party-dress stage, about the age of Rachel's little sister Billie. Not that I ever got much chance to wear a party dress. And even less, since Peter's accident and illness.

To give him his due, Dad does try though to do the best for me as well as Peter. So I said, "Oh, I don't want anything special, Dad. Just a meal out in a restaurant, or something like that."

Well, I couldn't say how much I longed for a real

party, with loads of my mates and nice music and everyone just chilling and having fun. And me at the centre of it all. That sounds very selfish and maybe it was. But I longed, just for once, to have nothing to worry about but celebrating and having a good time.

Dad looked relieved. "Well, that can be arranged. I'll book a table somewhere nice." He hesitated again, and added, "Maybe you'd like to ask a friend along. Just one. Any more would make Peter a bit edgy, I think . . ."

I thought, no way! I knew just how it would be. Dad trying his best to be jolly and like an ordinary family, Peter picking at his food and hardly speaking if he was down, or making bitterly sarcastic comments. Me trying to smooth things and pretend to be enjoying myself. I wasn't inflicting that on any of my friends. So I said, "I'd rather it was just the three of us really, Dad."

And he looked relieved again.

Peter was having a particularly down spell just then. Dad had trouble getting him to school some days. But if he stayed home, he'd just lie on the bed staring at the ceiling as often as not. It was really beginning to get to me. I felt it must show too, because there were times when the girls seemed to act a little odd around me. For instance, the Saturday Peter was in hospital again for tests and Dad and I visited him. The girls had all gone off shopping together. Nothing unusual in that – we often went into the city on a Saturday. But it seemed odd that they *all* went, even Annie, the new member of our group. And I was sure something had happened that day that nobody was telling me about.

"It *was* a weird kind of day," admitted Amber. "For a start, that Mark chatting up Holly. And then Willow almost taking money from Annie's purse. (Willow had already told me about that episode.) And the trouble we had on the bus, getting the ba . . ." She stopped suddenly and her face went pink.

"The trouble with what?" I asked.

"The trouble with the boys on the bus," she said quickly. "Getting them to shut up. Shouting and chanting, just because their stupid old team won. They really did my head in."

She'd meant to say something else, I was sure of it. But she wasn't telling. I felt my heart give a horrid flop. There were one or two other times I'd caught a couple of them talking and they'd shut up when they saw me. It really hurt. None of us ever had secrets from one another – except for mine. I wondered if Amber had said anything about Peter, but she'd never broken a promise before, and I had to believe it wasn't that.

Maybe they just didn't want me as a friend any more. I couldn't blame them really. Maybe I'm just not worth it, I thought, and it was then that the doubts about God's love began to creep in.

# *four*

The doubts were little ones at first, like wondering if God could really hear every single prayer uttered, let alone do something about them all. I wondered how he could possibly know whenever a bird falls down dead, or, most impossible of all, know exactly how many hairs there are on each head. I mean, not even your mum or your hairdresser would know that! For one thing, every person loses several hundred hairs every day and there are more growing all the time. How could anyone possibly keep count? It made my head spin.

Then I began getting the feeling that maybe God answered prayer for some people but that he certainly didn't answer mine. Maybe I didn't pray in the right way. Or long enough, or hard enough. Maybe I just wasn't worthy. Just too insignificant for God to bother with. Maybe it was just a complete load of rubbish that he loved me, or cared about me and about Peter. Maybe he didn't exist at all.

At Beech Bank, and in church, I'd heard Rod and Sadie say that it was okay to have doubts, or question our faith, or change in our feelings from day to day.

They said the thing to do was to talk about it, to bring things out in the open, that in fact it was good to ask questions and think things through. They encouraged us to go to them whenever we got fearful, or doubtful, or mixed up.

But I couldn't, and didn't. All by myself, I made up my mind that I didn't believe in God any more, that the Jesus stuff was all stories, and that if I wanted proof I only had to look at what had happened to Peter.

I dropped off going to church but still went to Beech Bank. For one thing, it was the only kind of social thing I had, and I'd have started climbing the walls if I'd had to stay in every evening. For another, it was where my friends were, and my friends really did care about me, even if God didn't. At least they seemed to, though I still had niggling little doubts that came up now and then. And I really did love them, no matter what they felt about me. Maybe I was getting paranoid as well as sad and bitter.

To prove to myself I was really liberated from any non-existent God, I decided to clear my room of all the "Christian" books I'd collected. I toyed with the idea of ceremonially burning them, but remembered that some were only borrowed from the Beech Bank library and not really mine. So I decided to sort them out – Beech Bank ones would go back there, the rest I would take to a charity shop. I got a couple of black bin bags and went to clear my crowded shelves.

Now, I had a huge collection of books, on shelves,

on top of the chest of drawers, on the window sill and piled in heaps on the floor. They were never very tidy, but now I noticed that they were even more higgledy-piggledy than usual. And there were gaps on the shelves which had been tightly crammed. A lot of the books were missing. And when I went to look closer, the missing ones were all Christian books, fiction or biographies or even some of the heavier teaching stuff.

What on earth was going on? Who'd taken the books? I knew it wasn't Dad – he left Peter's and my rooms strictly alone and we were grateful. We were supposed to keep them clean and tidy ourselves.

Who, then? Peter? But he only read sports mags and things like that, I thought. Not books and certainly not "God stuff".

Still – who else was there? I padded down the corridor and knocked on Peter's door. Usually he spent a lot of time in there, listening to moody music or playing mindless computer games or just lying on the bed brooding. All was quiet in there now, though. I pushed open the door and went in.

After Peter was diagnosed, Dad racked his brains for things to get him interested. One of the things he suggested was a complete makeover of Peter's room. He said Peter could choose the colour schemes, do the decorating and Dad would buy all new furnishings, carpets, new computer and music systems, all top of the range. Peter wasn't interested. But Dad kept on about it, so for the sake of peace Peter gave in and did the decorating. Not quite what Dad had envisaged though. Peter had chosen black – black walls, black bedding, even black carpet, which showed every bit of lint and ball of fluff horribly. Dad was dismayed, and I hated it. It gave me the creeps every time I saw it. I half-expected to see bats hanging from the curtain rail and spider's webs draped over the mirror.

Peter wasn't there, but I saw what I was looking for almost at once. A stack of books by the bed, tumbling untidily over the scruffy black carpet. My books. I stood there feeling a bit stunned. What was going on? And then a door slammed downstairs, there were feet on the stairs and Peter was bursting into the room, in a tracksuit and trainers, his hair damped with sweat. His jaw dropped when he saw me. "What are you doing in here?"

I thought it best to come clean. I pointed to the books and said, "Looking for my stuff. My books."

"Oh – yeah." He looked slightly embarrassed, picked up a towel and began to rub his head and face vigorously. All this seemed rather strange. Peter used to train and exercise, but he hadn't done so for ages.

"Have you been out running?"

"Yeah. Bit out of condition though." He draped the towel round his neck and rummaged for a clean T-shirt. "Sorry about the books. Should have asked first."

"That's okay." My brother seemed different

somehow, colour in his cheeks, almost cheerful. I trod
cautiously. "Did you read them?"

Peter was pulling the sweaty tracksuit top over his
head. His voice was muffled. "Yeah. Some of them.
Quite a few."

His head came out of the top and he flung the top
into the corner. He looked at me.

"Clo, something's happened." I held my breath,
praying silently – oh, please God – although I don't
believe in you any more – please let it be good.

"Yeah, well, since you got this Christian thing
you've been different. More – peaceful somehow.
Less edgy – even around me. Like – like – you've got
something inside you that helps – " He broke off,
embarrassed again. My heart was thumping hard. He
went on, "Anyway, I thought I'd have a look at those
books you read. See if I could work it out."

I didn't say a word. I couldn't believe what I was
hearing. "Anyway, some of those life-stories got to
me, like that guy who'd been a drug runner and gang
leader. And one who'd murdered someone. And that
one on Death Row. I thought – well, if God can change
people like them – and people like my little sister –
then maybe he can change me."

Suddenly his face blazed with something that came
from deep inside him, something that was new and
real and joyful. "And he has, Clo! I prayed a prayer
that's in one of the books, and it's happened! Jesus
is real and he's in my life! It's all gonna be different!

He might even make me well again – but even if he doesn't, I know he has some plan for me and it's a good one. I'm gonna start living again!"

He grabbed his clean clothes and headed for the bathroom, slamming the door. I heard the shower start up and another sound I hadn't heard for ages – Peter humming a tune as he threw off the rest of his clothes.

I stood in the middle of my brother's horrid black room and the tears began to pour down my face. I said, over and over, "Thank you, God. Thank you, God. Thank you."

I had my miracle.

## *five*

It was as though a huge dark cloud that had hung over our house for the last couple of years was suddenly lifted. We could see the sun and breathe fresh air and listen to the birdsong again.

Peter was so different. He went to school every day, saw some of his old friends, did some sport, talked and even laughed. He still had his down moments, but they didn't last long. And when I peeked into his room a few days later, I found that it was transformed. There were some bright posters on the wall and a different duvet cover in red and gold. And the black walls were now covered with gold and silver stars, the ones you stick on and that shine in the dark. There were even some on the ceiling, each one like a tiny sparkling symbol of the new hope that Peter had discovered.

It was so awesome that I could hardly take it in. Dad was mystified (poor man, his kids were proving to be a great puzzle to him) but pleased, cautiously, because he hoped it wouldn't be just another phase that would soon fizzle out. He warned me privately to be prepared for Peter to take another sudden down turn.

I didn't think he would, because what had happened was nothing that could be explained, humanly speaking. It was all to do with God. And God never changes, whatever we think or feel, he always stays the same.

Peter said he was thinking of coming to church with me and he did, the next Sunday morning, which had all the girls in a twitter, because they hadn't seen much of him before. I'd warned them to take it easy, not to crowd him, and they were cool about that.

It didn't even burst my bubble when Dad mentioned, a day or two before my birthday, that he'd had to change the date of my birthday dinner. Something had come up, he said, which I assumed meant a mix-up with the booking. We'd make it the following evening instead.

"That's okay, Dad," I said, and really meant it.

My birthday morning was a lovely sunny day,

and for once I didn't even think wistfully about big celebrations. There were cards and presents from the family, including a big parcel from Peter that contained all new gear, cool new jeans in just the right size and the style I like, a jade-green sparkly top, even a pair of strappy sandals that I loved on sight. And bling – dangly jade-green and silver stuff from Peter, but the real thing from Dad – a chunky bracelet with a fine etched pattern and a little safety chain that I knew was solid silver. I was amazed that Peter had gone shopping for me. Last year I'd not even had a card from him. They'd gone to a lot of trouble and I was touched.

At school, there were more cards and little gifts from the girls – pretty stationary, toiletries, a velvet belt (Willow!), paperbacks. Lots of hugs and kisses. I felt a lump in my throat. I'd only been imagining that they'd cooled off towards me. They seemed really excited that it was my birthday.

"Doing anything this evening, Clo?" Peter asked as we walked home from the school bus.

"Well, seeing as the dinner is tomorrow, I'll go down to Beech Bank with the others," I said. "Friday night is usually good – everyone stays late and sometimes we cook up sausages or something."

"Maybe I'll walk down with you," said Peter.

I was surprised, and felt it only fair to give him a warning. "Most of the guys there are a bit younger than you."

"Still – maybe I'll check it out."

Dad had ordered a Chinese takeaway with all my favourite dishes. I was quite enjoying my birthday for once.

"Why don't you put on your new gear?" suggested Peter as we were clearing the empty foil dishes into the recycling bin.

I felt my eyebrows go up. "What – for Beech Bank? Won't I look a touch overdressed?"

"It's your birthday, isn't it?"

To please him, I got myself all togged up in the new stuff, bling and all. It did make me feel like a million dollars, although the sandals were a bit killing for walking, so I took them in a bag and wore my old flats.

Beech Bank seemed a bit quiet when we arrived. Lights were on in the kitchen and the side rooms, but the big room was all in darkness. Not many people about either. I wondered where everyone was.

"It's usually a bit livelier than this," I said apologetically to Peter as I changed my shoes in the lobby.

"Maybe it'll liven up later," said Peter. He sounded rather strange. I wondered if he was nervous about being here, among Christian people.

"Everybody's really cool, you'll see – " I began to say, when suddenly the building seemed to explode.

The double doors of the big room flew open and all the lights went on in a sudden blaze of brilliance. Dozens of heads popped up and dozens of voices yelled at the full pitch of their lungs, "SURPRISE! Happy Birthday Chloe!" and launched into a round of "Happy Birthday to You"!

Then people were surrounding me and hugging me and jumping up and down. Over their heads I saw Peter grinning and giving me the thumbs-up, and I realised that he'd been in on this too. It fairly took my breath away!

Beyond the mass of bodies, all dressed to the nines in party gear, I glimpsed a magical transformation. The little red bistro tables were dressed up with tall silver candles and white posies and silver spangles on the cloths, huge red and silver balloons swung and floated ceilingwards, a big banner stretched right across the end of the room proclaimed "HAPPY BIRTHDAY CHLOE". Party poppers were already popping and throwing out yards of shiny red streamers which festooned themselves over the chairs and tables and people's heads. A big trestle table laid with a delicious-looking buffet stood against one wall and another table held a pile of brightly-wrapped parcels, large and small, or long or mysteriously lumpy.

Seeing my eyes on it, Holly said, "All for you," and Rachel said, "You didn't think those tiddly little things were your *real* presents, did you?"

I didn't know what to think. My head was spinning. My favourite music was playing and all my friends were here. They'd done all this for me. They loved me that much.

Tears filled my eyes, and for a moment the whole scene became a watery blur of silver and red. Sadie was beside me, giving me a kiss and a comforting squeeze. "Enjoy the evening, Chloe. A special event for a special person."

And that was how I felt, for the first time in ages. Special. Because all these people loved me and God loved me too. Although I'd turned my back on him, he'd stuck by me and answered my prayers for Peter in ways I'd never dreamed. I belonged to him, and he would never leave me.

I hugged Sadie back, and then someone was turning up the music and shouting "Hey! Let's party!" and suddenly the tears were gone and I was ready to laugh and sing and dance, because today was my birthday, and it had turned out to be the best one ever.

## Mystery in the Snow
## by J. M. Evans

Not long after solving their first mystery (*The Treasure Hunt*), Ravi, Debbie, Lance and Joel find themselves with another problem; Ravi's shed has been burgled. Can they find out who did it? The plot thickens as an old lady's handbag goes missing, then a cat disappears. Can all these things be connected? Join the Christian friends as they find answers in unexpected places. For ages 8–11.

"So exciting that I couldn't put it down!" – Lydia

ISBN 978 0 9536963 3 8

*Find all these and more at* www.dernierpublishing.com *Also available from your local book shop and on-line book store.*